THE O'MALL . . CRIME
THRILLERS

STILL WATERS

AN O'MALLEY & SWIFT NOVEL
BOOK 8

K.T. GALLOWAY

To my readers… for getting O'Malley & Swift to eight books!!!!

Wow!

I couldn't do it without you, thank you.

THE EIGHTH INSTALMENT IN THE BESTSELLING O'MALLEY AND SWIFT CRIME THRILLER SERIES!

Still waters run deep

In the midst of a local New Year's Eve celebration a teen boy emerges from the legendary Lowanford Lake. Missing for nearly a week, his skin bloated and covered in sores from the water, it's a miracle he's alive.

The legend weaves stories of the lake's miraculous waters—warm and luminescent—possessing the power to heal all afflictions.

But the legend is soon questioned when the next day a body floats to the surface.

And when another teen boy goes missing, Annie and Swift are up against the clock to find him before he succumbs to the water too.

The eighth and most unsettling instalment yet in one of the hottest new crime series, perfect for fans of JD Kirk, LJ Ross, Alex Smith, J M Dalgliesh, and Val McDermid.

MAILING LIST

Thank you for reading STILL WATERS
(O'Malley & Swift Book Eight)

While you're here, why not sign-up to my reader's club where you be the first to hear my news, enter competitions, and read exclusive content:

Join KT Galloway's Reader Club
at ktgallowaybooks.com

ONE

SUNDAY

MAISIE COOPER ALWAYS KNEW WHEN SHE WAS ABOUT to be told off. Her mum had a face that told a thousand stories and none of them were really suitable for children. In a mundane town like Lowan, with more wild rabbits than people and a non-existent nightlife, Maisie's mum's face was as exciting as it got. But mostly, it was a warning beacon for Maisie and her twin brother, Aaron, to catch the school bus before she kicked off at them for spilling cereal or not making their beds.

That evening, as the three of them had headed out to the playing fields for the New Year's Eve celebrations, her mum's face was telling the tale of ancient Italy and the imminent eruption of Vesuvius. Which is

1

why Maisie found herself sneaking off to the woods when she was distracted by Valerie from the local store, stopping to ask for signatures on a petition to ban Morrisons from building on the outskirts of town. As she slipped away into the darkness of the night, Maisie felt like telling Valerie she was wasting her time. Her mum had smiled twice this year and one of those times had been because of Morrisons.

"You'd better not be gate-crashing my party," Aaron said, sneaking up beside Maisie and making her jump.

"I was going this way anyway." Maisie glared at her brother and carried on towards the woods. These days Aaron was always two steps ahead. The idea of walking with Maisie now they'd hit their teen years was horrifying to him. "You can't stop me."

"God, you're so embarrassing," Aaron scoffed, walking faster.

Maisie dug the toe of her boot into the wet grass and watched as Aaron disappeared between the trees. She knew she was embarrassing; she didn't need her stupid brother to keep telling her. It was the reason she had no friends. Who'd want to hang out with Maisie and her damp-riddled house and her angry mum and her annoying brother? Not when there were girls who had the latest phones and trainers without holes in them in her new school. Maisie hated high school, that's when it had all gone wrong. The gulf between the Coopers and the rest of the teens had grown into a chasm. Her mum had lost the final glimmer of light. Aaron had stopped liking her. At primary, Maisie used to count down the hours until school was over; now she hated school, but she had no reason to want to be at home either.

A flash of light shone through the trees. A mobile. Then another. Maisie's brow scrunched. Aaron wasn't alone in the woods. She crept forward as silently as she could until she was under the cover of the trees too. Despite the full moon and only a stark cover of branches, it was so dark that Maisie couldn't see where she was putting her feet. The holes in her trainers had already let in the dampness from the grass, she didn't want to get splinters too. But the call of whatever her brother was up to was too great. Maybe she *would* go and crash his party.

The lights swung back and forth up ahead, shining the way for Aaron and whoever he was with. He walked around the outskirts of the trees and then vanished at the head of the green space. Maisie followed as close behind him as she dared. Though she knew these parks as well as she knew her own back garden, having played out here her whole life, she knew small streams and fords were running in the same direction. It wasn't a cold night, given they were supposed to be in the depths of winter, but Maisie didn't fancy tripping headfirst into running water.

Voices caught on the air. Maisie held her breath to listen, her heart hammering too loudly. It was Aaron and the other voices were his friends. She didn't like it when he was with his friends. They made him meaner. They laughed at people who were different. They taunted the younger kids at school. And through the sounds of her own breathing, Maisie could hear them jeering at something and it pinched at a ball of anxiety in her chest.

Have they seen me?

She backed behind one of the larger trunks and held her breath, waiting for them to find her and do their worst. Sticks and stones and all that, though Maisie knew the words hurt harder than the thumps. A minute passed, then another. It wasn't until the chill started to creep in through her jacket that Maisie realised they weren't laughing at her. Shivering, she pulled her jacket tighter, wincing at the pain in her cold fingers as they creaked to work. She peeked out, the crowd of five teens glowed with the glare of their mobiles, her brother in the middle. One of the boys pushed at Aaron's shoulder, causing him to stumble. Aaron laughed, but Maisie could tell by his face he wasn't happy about it. Another boy snatched at Aaron's phone, turning it over in his hands, yelling something that was caught in the trees and didn't quite reach back to his sister. But she could guess what it was because the girls did it to Maisie too. The Coopers didn't use their phones for show, they called and messaged and occasionally took photos, but the memory was minuscule, and the pictures pixelated. Every birthday and Christmas, Maisie hoped for a new one and then had to pull on a smile when she opened yet another hand-knitted

4

something or second-hand board game with pieces missing.

"Give over," Aaron shouted, pushing back against the boys as they crowded around him.

They broke away, laughing, but something set the hair on the back of Maisie's neck alight. Maybe it was the way they were tackling her twin brother around the neck, or the elbow to the ribs masked as harmless. She knew it was the mark of a teen boy, but she felt everything Aaron felt, and it wasn't a nice mixture of fear and anger.

Without thinking, Maisie pushed away from the tree and started to stride towards the boys, her fists clenched in her palms. But before they'd even noticed her, they turned and started walking deeper into the trees, dragging Aaron with them. He could have slipped away if he wanted to, but Maisie could feel the tug of camaraderie keeping him with his friends.

"If that's what friends are like then I'm glad I don't have any," she whispered, slowing down and following them from a distance.

They cut a path through the trees, illuminating the way with their phone torches, Maisie not far behind. They wound through the bare branches, still making fun of each other, the occasional taunt reaching her ears. They'd moved away from Aaron and were teasing one of the others about his mum, or maybe it was his sister. Either way, Maisie didn't want to hear what they were saying, it made her face heat and her head itch. She pulled up her hood and smothered their voices. They walked for another few minutes until the trees gave way to the body of water that their stupid town was known for. Lowanford Lake.

Locals loved to rave about its luminescence and the unusual warmth. She'd learnt about it in one of her science classes, but like everything else in Maisie's life, remembering useless information was too hard. Most classes she just scraped by, but some were harder than others, and those were the ones with the scores of writing and words she didn't understand. Numbers. That's what she liked. But the lake had no numbers, just words.

The five boys fell through the trees and ran down to the water's edge, shoving at each other, tripping over their own feet on the shingle. The water glowed softly, lighting the shore brightly enough that they pocketed their phones and could still see what they were doing. Maisie tucked herself behind a tree and watched, her stomach a bubble of acid.

"Dare you," one of them yelled.

"No, you go, it's your turn," another yelled back.

They jostled some more, pushing each other towards the water. Aaron held back and the fear growing in Maisie was apparent on Aaron's face. He couldn't swim, neither of them could, so even paddling in the water could be dangerous. What if he slipped and fell or someone pushed him too deep?

Like sharks circling prey, the boys must have picked up on Aaron's nerves and they turned their attention in his direction.

"I can't be bothered to get wet," he shrugged, making out like it was a waste of time.

"Chicken?" "Loser." "That's not what we heard."

The taunts came thick and fast and made Maisie's head spin. Two of the boys had linked their arms through Aaron's and were helping him towards the lake, their laughter cutting into Maisie like a knife. Aaron's pleas turned quickly from the casual to something altogether more frightened. She needed to do something, and she needed to do it quickly. They were nearing the edge of the lake, the water lapping at Aaron's trainers.

Maisie bit into her lip, the pain sharp, giving her the shock she needed to take action. Above them the crack bang of the New Year's Eve firework show had started, showering the sky with lights and drowning out the cries of her brother.

Bang.

Bang.

Bang.

Maisie covered her ears and ran out onto the shore.

"Hey," she shouted. "Leave him alone."

The fireworks covered her shouts as they bloomed around the stars, reflecting in the glow of the water. She was nearly there. Nearly at the boys. Though she had no idea what she was going to do when she reached them.

And that's when she saw it.

Out of the corner of her eye, a movement so

smooth she didn't register it to start with. Blending in with the rockets and strobes flickering on the surface of the water, there was something in the lake and it was coming in their direction. It moved towards them all, slowly at first, then as it emerged more from the water it started to speed up. It was grotesque. Human-like in stature, but bloated, grey, covered in sores, skin dripping from its arms and chest.

Maisie heard a scream, loud, piercing through the gaps in the fireworks like the whizz of a Catherine Wheel. Only this wasn't the sound of ignited gunpowder it was the sound of fear. Her own fear. The boys turned to look at where the sound was coming from.

"Maisie," Aaron yelled, the grip of his friends loosening. "What the… what the hell are you doing?"

They focussed on Maisie, then one by one turned to see what it was she was screaming about, stilling like statues when they caught sight of the horror. It was nearly out of the water now, completely naked with skin the colour of a new bruise. Maisie drew in a breath and the air around the lake fell into an eerie silence, her ears popping with the force of it. She stumbled backwards, losing her balance as the boys took off and pushed past her to get to the relative safety of the woods and the crowds of adults on the other side.

"Aaron," she cried. "Get up Aaron."

The boys had dropped him at the edge of the lake, keen to get away. But he wasn't moving, paralysed with what was going on around them, just as much as Maisie was. She could feel it in them both. A deep, gut-wrenching punch of fear that poisoned her blood and weakened her bladder.

"Get up, get up, get up," she yelled, her voice reedy over the rush of sounds in her ears.

But it was too late. As the figure took its last step out of the lake and bent down over her brother, Maisie fell to the floor, a pool of warmth spreading through her jeans. And as her brother cried out for help, Maisie's mind went black.

TWO

MONDAY

"WHAT DO YOU MEAN, WE CAN'T HAVE PARTY poppers?" Annie grimaced as Swift leant over her and drew a black line right through *party poppers* on her list. "What's a party without party poppers?"

"A grown-up party, for a start," Swift replied. "But since when were party poppers a good idea in a police station? You yell *surprise* and pull one of those and all of a sudden you're surrounded by armed police who were just trying to enjoy their breakfast."

He made a small explosion noise and gestured with his hands to go with it.

"Fair point," Annie conceded. "But let's have some for her party party, not her work party."

Swift sighed and pushed his chair back from his

desk. "I need a coffee," he said, leaving the open plan office without asking Annie if she would like one too.

Annie ignored him, turned back to her list, and wrote *party poppers* back at the bottom. Swift was always a grump before coffee, everyone knew that. And organising a party at 6 am on a Monday morning wasn't Swift's idea of fun. So, it was a good job he hired Annie to be part of the Major Crime Unit or there would be no surprise birthday party and Tink might quit through the lack of respect from her peers. Doubtful, but Annie was running out of ideas to persuade Swift that it was a good thing they were doing.

The Major Crime Unit, or MCU, was as much Annie's family as her actual family. DI Joe Swift, a flower under his grumpy exterior, DC Tom Page, a muscly enigma, and DS Belle Lock, or Tink as her diminutive frame bestowed upon her. And Annie, not police, but an important part of the team, nonetheless. Trained as a psychotherapist, Annie O'Malley solved crimes on the basis that they were hinged together by the madness of people.

New Year's Day was generally quieter for the MCU. The crimes tended to be smaller, manageable by the uniformed officers out on the beat. Annie wondered if the criminals took the Christmas period off work and started their New Years with a list much like her own. Less glittery wrapping paper and more grievous bodily harm. Still, it didn't hurt to make

Tink's birthday a good one, given she'd be spending the day at her desk.

Annie doodled on the side of her pad as the office door opened and some of the officers from other teams started to arrive.

"Happy New Year," she said, smiling at the man who was tucked up warmly in what looked like a new coat and hand-knitted scarf.

There were a few different teams who shared the open plan office with the MCU. Annie didn't know them well, just to say hello and goodbye to, but they were all friendly enough. The door bashed open, and Swift blustered in, a coffee in each hand. *Well, most of them are friendly enough.* Annie rolled her eyes and took the proffered drink with a thanks. Flat white, just as she liked it. Swift sipped away on his black coffee and they fell into a comfortable silence as Annie subtly checked out the dark bags under her boss's eyes.

"Everything alright, Swift?" she asked. "Busy Christmas? Already regretting your New Year resolutions?"

Truth be told, Annie had hoped that Swift would have been around at Christmas so they could have seen each other. But he'd not been in touch since Christmas Eve except for a text the next morning wishing her a happy day. Annie pictured him rattling around on his own in his giant house like Scrooge, but something about him this morning was making her question if he'd been busy doing something else.

Something that involved alcohol and a gathering of other people.

Swift leant forward on his elbows, leaning in towards Annie. She caught a whiff of a new after-shave, very different to his usual citrus number.

"Annie," he said, conspiratorially, "what did you mean by party party. I thought we were hosting a surprise bash here next week. Cake, present, a cup of tea, *surprise*. Boom, bash, done. Back to work."

"And we are," Annie said, sitting back in her chair. "But I thought it might be nice to do something else, too. A proper party rather than trying to shovel in a piece of Colin Caterpillar in between solving crimes."

"Colin who?" Swift raised an eyebrow. "And where were you planning on hosting this extra party for a woman who is still in her twenties and probably doesn't want to sit around drinking Cava with a bunch of oldies like us for her birthday? Organised fun, Annie. It's just not it."

Annie sighed, taking in what Swift had just said. Tink was young and cool and probably had loads of things already organised.

"You're right," she said. "I was just trying to be nice, but I guess not everyone grew up with no friends and needs their elders to sort them out."

She propped her elbow on the desk and leant her chin on her hands, feeling Swift's hand on her back.

"Not everyone had a dad who absconded with only one of his daughters, leaving the other one behind with a mum who turned out to be an under-cover police officer who killed a man," Swift whispered. "How is Mim?"

Annie couldn't help but chuckle at the extreme-ness that surrounded her early years. She'd been seventeen when her dad had kidnapped her sister, Mim and it was only last year that the two women had reunited. It had been great for Annie to connect with Mim, but it had brought about more questions than answers. Annie's dad running from Annie's mum for starters. There had never been a kidnapping, only a father protecting the only child he could at the time.

"I was thinking more about my lack of personal style and the inability to not say what I was really thinking as a child, but yeah, all that too." Annie looked over at Swift, their eyes catching, her chest constricting.

She looked away and gathered her coffee mug in her hands, lifting it to cover her face. Over the last two years, Annie and Swift had grown closer than she'd expected they would. It was a difficult situation because he was her boss, she was still relatively new to the team, and she loved her job too much to jeopardise it. Annie had stayed at Swift's house when she'd broken her ankle, he'd looked after Sunday the stray cat when Annie had gone on holiday, they'd protected each other in the face of danger never once even questioning the reasons why they did it. All of those encounters had cemented their friendship as one that would see through the test of time. The only thing left was for Annie to tell Swift how she really felt about him, but when moments like *that* just happen on a day-to-day basis, Annie would rather face Bubonic Plague again than risk Swift never looking at her.

"Maybe I could do something at mine," he said, his voice gravely. "Just something small, mind. A few drinks."

"And some party poppers?" Annie added, smiling.

Swift laughed and shook his head. "O'Malley, I have to draw the line somewhere."

"Draw it after the party poppers, it'll be worth it, I promise," she said, holding his gaze for a beat too long.

"It had better be worth it." Swift spun around on his chair and started tapping away at his keyboard, a redness spreading up his neck.

"What had better be worth it?" Annie and Swift looked up from the screens to Tink bustling through the door. "Happy New Year guys, did you have a good one?"

The young sergeant looked between them as if waiting for a joint answer, such was the obviousness of Annie's feelings to everyone but Joe Swift. Pulling her hat from her head, Tink ruffled life back into her pixie cut and shrugged her coat from her shoulders.

"Quiet one with Sunday," Annie said, looking back down at her keyboard.

"Annie!" Tink plonked herself down at her desk opposite and pushed her screen low so she could get a better angle for her disapproving face. "You're in your thirties and you spent New Year's Eve with your cat."

Annie felt her face heat again. "Mim's away with work."

Tink turned her disapproval to their boss. "Swift, what were you doing and why didn't you invite Annie?"

"It's fine, Tink, Sunday is good company." Annie shot her a look.

"Better than Swift?" Tink replied, scowling in the DI's direction.

"Sometimes," Annie said, grinning. "What did you do?"

"Went to an underground rave and got drunk and debaucherously crazy."

"Usual Sunday night for you then, Tink?" Swift muttered, waving hello to DC Tom Page as he took his seat next to Tink, bringing with him the cold from the outside.

"Happy New Year, team MCU," Page said gleefully across their small bank of desks. "Can I get anyone a coffee, tea, hot chocolate, Bucks Fizz?"

"You're in a good mood," Swift said, lifting his eyes from his screen. "Were you at Tink's rave too?"

Page opened his mouth to answer but was cut short by DCI Robins' shadow darkening the desks.

"Welcome back, detectives," she said, her immaculate dark bob as neat as ever. "I'm afraid the frivolities will have to wait for another time. We've got a live one and it's juicy. My office in ten."

"Looks like the criminals are starting on their own resolutions early doors this year." Annie finished her coffee and held out her mug to Page. "Ten minutes is time for another, thanks Tom."

Page took the mug and lifted Swift's from his desk. "It's my resolution to pass my sergeant's exam this year, and making hot drinks is top of that agenda."

"Mine is to worry less," Tink said, before adding. "Green tea, please Page."

"Green?" Swift said, nose wrinkled.

"It's better for me, caffeine makes my heart race."

"Green tea would make my heart stop." Swift looked disgusted. "A racing heart is what gets me up in the morning."

"Oh eye?" Tink winked at him.

"Shut up, Tink," Swift grumbled. "You know what I meant."

"I'd say, judging on your eye bags, I know exactly what you meant," she said, blowing him a kiss and offering to help Page.

Swift looked across the desk to Annie as Tink and Page bundled out of the double doors in search of some low-caffeine green tea. He seemed to want to say something, opening and closing his mouth a couple of times as he tried to settle on the right words.

"It's okay," Annie said, putting him out of his misery. "I'm used to spending holidays on my own, I quite like it after the busyness of the year. I hope you did have a good one, though. Ended 2023 with a bang?"

"You could say that," Swift replied. Annie waited for him to expand on why, but no explanation was forthcoming.

One of her resolutions for the New Year was to be brave. Annie knew that living in an office-cum-flat wasn't sustainable forever and she had to be brave to find somewhere else to live. She also had to muscle up some courage to ask DCI Robins for an extension on her contract or to make it permanent. Since starting with the MCU, Annie had been on regular contract work as a psychotherapist, she now needed a regular income if she was going to get a mortgage on a new place. But she didn't want to rock the boat in case Robins realised she wasn't an integral part of the team and cancelled the recurring job she had in place. Annie watched as Swift rubbed his hand over the back of his neck and bit his lower lip, she was going to ask him to help her do the bravest task of all this year, but now she wasn't sure she dared. Somewhere, hidden behind password-protected software, were the archives. Hidden amongst the cold cases and the centuries-old crime files was a folder with informa-tion on her mum. Annie needed to find it and read it and work out once and for all whose side she was on. But she wasn't sure she could do it alone. Looking at Swift, she wasn't sure he could help her now either.

THREE

TEN MINUTES LATER THE FOUR MEMBERS OF THE
MCU were crowded around DCI Robins' desk,
staring at a picture of what looked like the Creature
from the Black Lagoon.

"Jeez Tink, can you shuffle that way a bit, prefer-
ably out the door? Your tea smells worse than O'Malley's cat on a good day." Swift rolled the wheels of
his chair as far from Tink as physically possible
without ending up in Page's lap.

"Oy, I'll have you know that Sunday smells
delightful these days," Annie shouted from where she
was leant on the corner of Robins' desk.

"And I'll have you know this tea is a mixture of
nettle and liquorice and will help me focus whilst also
keeping me calm," Tink muttered, sipping at the
green liquid with a wince. "I'd be a crap detective if I
couldn't focus, wouldn't I?"

"It'll help you focus on your P45 if you don't put

a lid on it." Swift looked as grassy as the tea and Annie stood up to give herself room in case he was about to throw up all over Robins' desk. "And I'd be a crap detective if I couldn't work out from your face that you hate it as much as I do."

"Are you all quite finished?" the DCI said staring at the team and the room fell into a fuzzy silence.

Page lifted an arm in the air and cleared his throat. "Can it be noted that I'm not part of this conversation, I'm ready to listen?"

Swift snorted. "Alright Page, no need to drop us in it, Robins here doesn't have the power to grant you your sergeants' badge just because you're behaving."

"But I've got the power to remove all of yours, inspector. DC Swift has quite a ring to it." Robins rolled her eyes and lifted the photographs from the desk to hand around. "If you're all ready to start work now, please. I don't know what's gotten into you this morning. You're like bickering siblings at Christmas and there's another 359 days to go before we're back there again."

She handed the photos to Annie. Screenshots from a mobile phone video, grainy and dark. Annie twisted it sideways to make out the mass of figures lying in a pile on the shore by a lake and her stomach twisted as she realised it wasn't a mass of figures at all.

"Oh god," she said, handing the picture on to Tink as quickly as she could, rubbing her hands on her trousers. "Who is that? What happened to them?"

Robins waited until the team had all seen the

20

photo before she spoke. A new kind of silence had descended on the office that felt as palpable as the stench of Tink's tea.

"That is Leon Scutts, eighteen," Robins started, spinning another photo on her desk to face the team. A teenage boy smiled back at them; happy, cheeky, with the looks of someone who would break a few hearts when he grew up. "Was missing from his hometown of Lowan for five days before he turned up looking like this."

"Where had he been?" Annie asked, gesturing for the photo back from Robins. "He looks like he is already in the later stages of decomp."

Robins hummed at Annie, nodding. "You'd think so, wouldn't you?"

Annie looked closer at the photo. The body of Leon Scutts was bloated beyond recognition. His naked skin almost navy, sagging and limp as though it was melting from his bones. The only part of the teenage boy that was remotely human was his face. It looked nothing like the photo of the smiling, happy schoolboy, but there were elements that reminded Annie she was looking at a person.

"What do you mean?" Swift asked, glancing over Tink to the picture in Annie's hands. "Has Evans worked his magic yet?"

Evans was the hospital pathologist who worked closely with the MCU. Robins shook her head at the question. "That's the thing," she said. "Leon isn't dead. Last night he walked out of the lake as though he'd just been for a swim. Nearly killed two bystanders by giving them a heart attack, brother and sister by all accounts."

"He walked?" Page spluttered. "Holy Moly. How?"

"Adrenaline," Robins replied. "And a whole lot of drugs."

"Drug, drugs?" Tink asked.

Robins shook her head. "Pain killers mostly. Codeine."

"How do you know this, is he able to talk?" Annie looked down at the boy in the photo, not under-standing how he could be alive when his whole body looked like a grape.

"He's currently in an induced coma in the ICU," Robins went on. "The nurses did bloods on admit-tance, and I expedited them. We don't know if he's going to come out of this or what he'll look like at the other end, so I need you guys to find out what happened to him."

"Do we have any idea at all?" Annie asked. "What about the mis-per file, any info on there? You said he'd been missing for five days?"

Robins shook her head again. "They only knew he was missing after the fact. Parents didn't file a mis-per, apparently. Uniform spoke to them at the hospital last night and Leon was supposed to be away on a trip with friends, so they weren't overly worried when they hadn't heard from him."

"Are they all accounted for?" Swift interrupted. "The friends?"

Robins tapped away at her keyboard, eyes narrowed. "Uniforms are on it this morning, but we've had no new missing persons filed and the news about Leon will have already spread around the parents."

"A lot of them might be hung over and not checking social media and messages." Tink sipped her tea again.

"Of course, I've got a team of uniform visiting those families first thing this morning." Robins ran a hand through her bob. "There is something else too. Something weirder."

"Weirder than a body that looks like *that* being able to walk unaided out of a lake?" Swift asked, glancing at the photo of Leon.

"Lowanford Lake," she began, tapping the body of water behind Leon in the picture. "Well known, as lakes go, because of the glowing algae. That's what makes it look like something out of The Twilight Saga or Zone, depending on your preference for teenage sci-fi. But the water is also a few degrees warmer than your average lake and legend has it that it holds healing properties."

"Not if Leon's anything to go by," Page muttered, wafting his hand in the direction of Robins' desk and the gruesome photo.

"I'm putting you all on this because you're the best team for it," Robins continued. "You've worked out cases stranger than this one, so hop to it. Swift, report back here first thing tomorrow, please. And try to keep your enquiries on the low down, we don't want a deluge of reporters at the scene as water is so volatile to get evidence from anyway."

"Guv," Swift said, pushing his chair back and opening the door to Robins' office. "Team, this way, please."

Annie stood, pulling Tink's chair out for her and letting her go first. They filed out one by one back to the open plan office and the chatter of the officers working and the angry shouts of Tink as Swift grabbed her mug and threw the contents in the fiddle leaf fig tree sitting innocently in the corner of the room.

"You'll kill it," Tink said, adding a few swear words under her breath.

"If it's good enough for you, it's good enough for the plant," Swift replied, but the look on his face made Annie chuckle.

That plant had been in the team for longer than a lot of the staff and it got special treatment, especially at Christmas. Rose, the station receptionist and Annie's best friend, used to be under strict orders to water regularly and feed it ground-up dead fish bones to keep the leaves strong and healthy. One slip up with the watering can and a few brown tips and Rose was stripped of her caring duties quicker than she could say Ficus Lyrata.

Swift deposited the file on Leon Scutts on his

desk and sank into his chair, spinning from side to side.

"Okay," he said, slapping his palms down on the table and making Annie jump. "This is unusual, granted. No dead body and all that."

"And we don't even know if a crime has taken place, with respect, sir," Tink interrupted.

"Fair point," Swift replied. "But I can't see why a teenage boy would do whatever *that* is to himself. But, you're quite right Tink. So let's gather as much information as we can and regroup here tomorrow. Page, I'm giving you more responsibility on this one, back up your sergeant's application with some solid fieldwork. I want you to go to the hospital and talk to Leon's parents. Find out more about the young lad; his likes and dislikes, hobbies, friends, girlfriends, boyfriends, anything you can to try and build a picture of him."

Page gave a salute and scribbled wildly on his notepad, tongue between his teeth.

"Tink, I need you to set up an incident room and then head to the hospital too. I need as much information on Leon's state as you can get from the nurses. Sweet talk them. Guilt trip them by telling them it's your birthday next week. Take biscuits. Anything to squeeze them of information about Leon's condition. I want to know why he's... blue, basically. Get a medical history from his files, if you can without a warrant, and detail any past episodes. Mental health too. Heck, tell me about any injuries even if it's a broken toenail."

Swift took a breath and turned to Annie.

"O'Malley," he said, gravely. "You're with me. I think we need to head to Lowan and check out the locals. Get a feeling for who lives there and what it's like for a teen boy to grow up in a small town that's only known for its warm water lake. As of now, there's no crime scene to talk of, we need to organise a uniform search to find out where Leon has been for the last five days and why he looks like he does."

"What are your first thoughts?" Annie asked, curious as to where the DI's mind was going.

Swift ran a hand over his face, flushing his cheeks pink. He looked more awake than he had earlier. Could have been the coffee, could have been the excitement of a new case.

"I think what we have is twofold. Firstly, that Leon is involved in something dangerous. And secondly, I think that teen boys don't have a lot of common sense. So it's a touch paper for something to go wrong. Other than that, I'm stumped." Swift slapped his hands on the desk again and sprang to his feet. "Right, let's get out there and get some answers because we're not going to get much solved sitting around talking. The game, as Sherlock so famously said, is afoot."

"Like the stench of Tink's tea," Page joked, grinning across at Tink.

Annie giggled, she couldn't help herself, the tea

had smelt like something unpalatable found growing under a toenail. Tink stuck her fingers up at Page, stood up, and started bundling her outdoor clothes back over her shirt and trousers.

"You won't be taking the mick out of me when it comes to chasing the bad guys and you're all too full of coffee and doughnuts to catch them," she said, pulling her hat down hard over her head. "Or when you keel over because your heart can't take the caffeine. Or when… oh sod it, I'm going to Maccy d's on the way to the hospital who cares about New Year's Resolutions when there's a sausage and egg McMuffin to shovel in your mouth?"

"Maybe some of us have picked resolutions that are easier to keep for longer than…" Swift looked at his watch. "Eight hours. Like not drinking god-awful tea."

Tink muttered under her breath and grabbed the files for the incident room, disappearing out the door with a huff.

"Case in point, "Swift said. "If that's what a lack of caffeine does to someone then hook it up to my veins. O'Malley, with me."

He marched to the door and held it open as Annie tripped over her feet to grab her coat.

Page whistled through his teeth. "Happy New Year, guys. Here's to a successful 2024!"

FOUR

"WHAT DID YOU AND MIM REALLY GET UP TO LAST night?" Swift asked as he pulled out of the station car park and put the heater on full blast. It didn't take long for the 4x4 to heat up and soon Annie was pulling at her scarf and loosening her zip. Her old Golf had a window that didn't quite shut properly so she was used to a permanent stream of air battering her head. This made a nice, warm change.

"What do you mean what did we get up to?" Annie asked, happy to pass the time.

Swift shrugged. "You know, it was New Year's Eve."

"It was," Annie agreed. She wondered if Swift pictured her out and about getting drunk with her friends like a normal thirty-something-year-old or spending it with family playing board games and charades by the fire. She thought about what she had actually been doing, her camp bed in the office she used as a flat, Miss Marple on ITVX on her laptop. She thought about her companion in the form of the giant orange cat she'd rescued last year who had curled up on her lap over the knitted blanket Mim had made for her for Christmas. She thought about the fact her sister and her cat were two of her only friends, and even her sister had deserted her for New Year. Annie didn't have old school friends because no one had wanted to befriend the weirdo whose Dad had absconded with her sister and left her behind. Rose, whom Annie had met at the station when she was working as a psychotherapist, had a new boyfriend and was otherwise engaged last night. So that was that. Annie had spent the night with a fat cat and an old lady sleuth.

She looked at Swift, studied the way he concentrated on the road with the tip of his tongue resting between his teeth. She wondered what he had been doing as the new year arrived and why he hadn't been in touch. It's not like they messaged a lot out of work, but she occasionally sent him a meme of a cat and he replied with a gif of another cat. Ever since they'd made it home in one piece from Majorca last summer, Annie felt like Swift had put up a DI barrier between them and she was having to chip away secretly at it like a prisoner at a brick wall to get back to how they'd been before.

"Mim is away with work, she left a couple of days ago," Annie went on. "So, I had a quiet one. Stayed up until midnight, made a toast to the beginning of

2024, promised myself I'd make some changes this year, fell asleep. Plus ca change, really."

"Oh." Swift slowed to take a roundabout, following signs to Lowan. "Right. I… sorry, I just thought…"

"That maybe I did something fun instead?" Annie interrupted.

Swift chuckled. "No, there's nothing wrong with being sensible, especially if that meant you didn't have to go out in the cold last night. It was bitter."

"You were out on the town then? Was it busy?" Annie's stomach twisted.

"No," Swift said, navigating the country roads carefully. "Not town, jeez Annie I'm way too old for that."

He didn't elaborate on where he *had* been and soon the car lulled into a comfortable silence as they passed through desolate farmland, with nothing to see except fields and more fields until a sign announced they were arriving in Lowan.

Lowan was a town stuck in the middle of nowhere. From a bird's eye view it would have the concentric circles of a tree stump; fields as the outer bark, then bypass, detached houses, council houses, playing fields, woodland, and then right in the centre was Lowanford Lake.

As they drove down the streets towards the lake where the uniformed officers were expecting them, Annie poured over the file and tried to digest the information that they'd been given. It wasn't a lot, and out here the connection was as iffy as Annie would expect in the middle of Norfolk farmland so she couldn't even Google the lake or stalk Leon on social media. Not that Annie did that much anymore, not with the kids anyway. They were all on TikTok or Snapchat and Annie couldn't work out how or why they worked. Still, Tink was building a picture of the young man and she could probably navigate her way around the apps because she was still under thirty. Leon Scutts was lucky to be alive and they needed to find out why luck was the only reason.

Swift pulled into a muddy carpark that backed onto a football field. Net-less goal posts flanked either end, the grass scrubby and bound to make play a little more interesting. A scattering of trees bordered the park, thickening to one side. Remnants of a night abandoned were laid on the muddy grass. Unlit fireworks, a trestle table with an urn and cups, a smoky bonfire.

Annie clambered out of the car as Swift turned off the engine, the frigid air immediately numbing her nose.

"Wow, it's cold. It's a good job my resolution is to be more resilient," Swift said, shutting the car door behind him and pulling his coat up around his chin.

Annie looked at him, eyebrow raised. "Resilient about what?" she poked.

Swift shrugged. "Let's go and find the lake."

You're infuriating, Joe Swift.

Annie skipped around the car and caught up with

the DI as he strode across the playing field towards the uniformed officers who had started to gather around the urn as though it would still be giving off heat, or the idea of it would be.

"DI Swift," Swift flashed his badge. "Annie O'Malley. What can you tell us?"

Annie waved at the two uniformed officers whose faces were a purple shade of cold even with their thick coats and gloves.

"PC Tooley, PC Sands, hi." the young woman said, indicating herself and her male colleague. "We just came over to see if there was any hot water left for a cuppa, we've been out here since last night and it's a bit cold."

She looked sheepishly at the urn and Annie felt for them.

"Why don't you tell us what you've found and then go and warm up? Get yourselves a proper hot drink. We'll be okay for an hour or so."

Annie saw Swift look at her out the corner of her eye, but she wasn't about to back down. These officers were kids themselves and it was bitterly cold. And as Robins had said, they had no idea where the initial crime scene was, or even if there was one yet, so there was nothing to protect and preserve.

"Thanks, O'Malley." PC Tooley smiled. "We've been doing door-to-door, but a lot of the town is still asleep and no one is answering. We did a sweep of the lake and the shore where Leon turned up, but there was nothing out of the ordinary... except Leon."

Annie looked at the clock on her phone. It was already just past nine, but it was New Year's Day and by the looks of the steam still rising from the urn it had been a late one, even if it had been abandoned.

"Did *anyone* talk to you?" Swift asked, his words clouding around his face.

Tooley struggled to unzip her breast pocket with the chunky gloves and pulled out a notebook.

"A couple of people were awake," she said, flicking it to the right page. "Thomas Windsor who runs the town museum…"

"This town has a museum?" Annie interrupted, looking around at the houses squatting beside the road. It was an in-and-out town, one where people didn't stop on the way through unless they lived there.

Tooley nodded. "It's mostly about the lake, apparently. But Windsor said we should check it out while we're here because there's some interesting items from when Lowan was a mining community. There's a lot of flint in the houses around here and it came from Lowan. Lowanford Lake is a pit lake. To be honest, even if the museum is as boring as it sounds, we were going to head there to warm up, weren't we Sands?"

"Yep," PC Sands said, joining in the conversation for the first time.

"So the lake is manmade," Swift asked. "Is that why it glows?"

"Not sure on that one yet, Guv," Tooley said. "It's

odd though, the way it glows. It's like something out of a movie."

"And it's warm too," Sands added. "Like, not warm warm, I wouldn't want to go in it. It's just not icy like you'd imagine a lake in the middle of the winter to be."

Swift nodded his thanks. "Off you go and defrost then, we'll have a look around and get back to you if we have any questions."

"Do you want to know about the other person we spoke to?" Tooley asked, looking at her notebook.

"Go on," Swift replied, stamping his feet.

"A Cameron Kirkpatrick," the young officer went on. "Doesn't live here, but he heard about what happened and arrived just after we did."

"He's keen," Annie said. "What do we know about him?"

"He lives in Norwich." Tooley's nose was bright red. "Runs a development business. He didn't say what his link was with Lowan, but all the farmland around the town just sitting there ripe for hundreds of houses is my main bet."

"Interesting," Swift said. "Thanks."

"Kirkpatrick disappeared not long after talking to us and Windsor lives above the museum, it's just off the high street."

Swift thanked the two young officers, and they headed off in the direction of their cruiser and hopefully some warmth.

"I thought you were going to tell me off for letting

them go," Annie said as she and Swift headed towards the tree line.

"Since when do I ever tell you off?" Swift replied, holding back a branch bare of leaves so Annie could pass by.

"Since never," she said, taking a moment to think about if Swift had ever given her any reprimands in their two years working together. "I don't think. But today could be the day to start."

"New year, new me?" he snorted. "Like you'd listen to me anyway. No, I was looking at you thinking what a difference it makes being with someone who cares about others, that's all. It's always your first thought; *how can I make it okay.*"

A tug of warmth spread through Annie's chest, but she didn't have time to relish in it before her police instincts kicked in. "Swift, what's that?"

They both stopped, looking at the mobile phone discarded on the woodland floor. It was half covered in leaves, just the glow of the screen illuminating it through the dusky light.

Swift rummaged around in his pocket and pulled out a pair of disposable blue gloves, snapping them over his bare hands. He crouched down, pushing the leaves away with a stick. Someone was calling the phone. Annie twisted her head around and read the name on the screen. *Aaron Cooper.* It rang out and the home screen came back into view.

"Didn't Robins say there was a brother and sister

out here last night when Leon appeared? Could be one of theirs?" Annie said."

"Yeah," Swift replied, picking the phone up and bagging it. "Aaron Cooper is the brother, he's currently in hospital being treated for shock, his sister is talking to officers in Norwich. But it looks like there was more than one teen boy out here last night, given the number of boobs on his home screen. We need to find out who they are and what they were doing out here. Let's get this checked for footage. Teens are surgically attached to their phones these days and whoever dropped this must have been in a hurry to not stop and look for it."

He dropped the bagged phone in his pocket and stood upright.

"Do you think this is some kind of teen prank gone wrong?" Annie asked as they continued on their way to the lake.

Swift hummed a noncommittal answer as his reply. "I don't know, O'Malley. Maybe. Teens are pretty clueless when it comes to safety."

"It's part of their DNA, brains aren't quite properly wired at that age," Annie said, stepping out past the trees to the shingle shore of the lake and stopping in her tracks. "Wow."

It was unlike anything she'd seen before. Even in the dusk of the morning, the water was luminescent, glowing like a snow globe that had just been shaken. Almost a perfect circle, Annie could see nearly all the way around, just a small section at the far end that was covered by the branches of a weeping willow was blocked from view.

"It looks almost magical," Swift said, dipping the toe of his boot in the water and sending a ripple out into the lake.

"It feels a bit eerie though, don't you think?" Annie asked, the skin on her arms rippling. There was something about the shadows cast up into the trees from the water that had Annie's senses working overdrive.

She couldn't put her finger on it, but there was something not right about Lowanford Lake. Not quite right about Lowan either.

FIVE

LOWANFORD LAKE MAY HAVE BEEN CHRISTENED WITH a boring name, but the lake itself was anything but. Despite her burgeoning sense of dread, Annie couldn't help being drawn to the water like a moth to a flame. She bent down, pulling off a glove and going against every grain in her body to dip her fingers in the water.

PC Sands had been right, the water felt warm to touch. It wasn't bath water warm, but against the freezing air it brought Annie's fingers back to life.

"What do you think makes it a few degrees above normal temperature?" Wiping her hand down her trousers she pulled her glove back on and shoved her hands in her pockets to preserve some of the trapped heat.

"Science was my worst subject at school," Swift said, poking the water with the same stick he'd poked at the leaves around the phone. "Maybe it's the algae?

Maybe it's the flint underneath it? I have no idea. I'm sure our Mr Windsor of the museum can tell us the answer to that one, though. What I'd like to know is if Leon Scutts' body looks like it does because he's spent the last few days *in* the lake. And if that's so, then how the bloody hell is he still alive?"

Annie had wandered around the edge of the lake as Swift had been talking. The shingle was clear, giving up no secrets. "It's not tidal, is it?" she asked, Swift now almost out of earshot.

"I don't think so, no." Swift jogged to catch up with her, his feet crunching on the stones. "Its man made and not connected to the other bodies of natural water that flow around Lowan, so I can't see how it will be tidal."

Annie poked at the stones with her boot. "Then it's not as though Leon could have been dragged into the lake from elsewhere, a river or whatnot."

"Nope," Swift said. "He would have had to go in at someplace around the shore. And... wait, what's that, O'Malley?"

Annie looked through the trees where Swift was looking. Yellow lights cut through the bare branches and Annie could see what looked like the outline of a small house.

"You think someone has been staying in there?" she asked as they both sped up and headed in the direction of the lights.

"I think someone is there now, and that's good enough for me. With winter trees and no foliage, they'd have the perfect view of the lake from that window."

Annie followed Swift away from the shoreline and into the woods. The low sun was burning a hole in the mist, waking the town of Lowan. Birdsong filled the sky now, the sweet flourish of a robin and the ever-present shouts of the seagulls despite being quite a few miles from the sea.

Whoever it was in the wooden shack masquerading as a house had a fire lit. Smoke billowed out the metal chimney stack thick enough to fill in the hole in the clouds burned by the sun.

"Keeping warm or burning evidence?" Annie asked, nodding to the plumes getting tangled in the tree branches.

Before Swift could reply, the sounds of feet hitting the shingle rang through the trees. Whoever it was, was running. And they were running fast. Swift moved in front of Annie, pushing her behind him with his arm as the footsteps quietened with the mulch underfoot in the trees.

"Show yourself," Swift shouted.

Annie tensed as the footsteps got closer.

"It's just me, guv." PC Tooley burst through the trees, her face bright red with the exertion of running.

"Tooley," Swift called, his shoulders sagging. "What on earth's happened?"

"You need to come with me, sir," she said, between pants. "Another boy is missing."

Swift looked over his shoulder at Annie and then

40

back to the young PC. "Who and where? We'll go now, but Tooley do me a favour and don't let whoever is in there leave before we can talk to them."

Tooley's brows drew together. "That's Freddie Mold's house. We tried him earlier. Looks like he's awake now. Don't worry, sir, he's on our list to talk to."

"He lives there?" Annie blurted.

Tooley nodded. "Apparently so. Kirkpatrick was telling us about him earlier. He's not going anywhere right now. And you both really need to come with me because this boy's parents look like they're about to lose the plot."

———

TOOLEY WASN'T KIDDING. SOMEHOW, THEY'D ALL ended up in the living room of an end terrace house overlooking the school. It had been a five-minute walk from the playing field, and they'd covered it in less than two. With a TV bigger than Annie's flat, two giant sofas facing it, and enough chintz to open a bric-a-brac shop Annie felt like she was going to end up in Swift's lap as she perched on the arm of one of the sofas. Swift had sent Tooley back to the woods to go and talk to the man who lived in the shack and Annie wished she'd got to go with her. Cold air and creepy woods were a lot easier to deal with than the petrified parents sitting opposite her and their equally petrified friends taking up most of the sofa next to Swift.

"I want you to talk us through what's happened. But first I need you to tell me your names and the name of your son so we can call it in." Swift asked, shifting slightly in Annie's direction.

The woman, presumably the boy's mother, tried to answer, but her voice was lodged in her throat. Her eyes were red, her face puffy, limp hair hung down her pale cheeks.

"Jacob Mortimore," the man said, taking the woman's hand in his. He was her polar opposite. His belly straining at his jumper, his neck blending into his chins. "I'm Carl, this is my wife Enid. Please find our son. He is our world."

At his words, Enid curled up into herself and sobbed into her chest. The woman sitting next to Swift lifted herself from the sofa and went to Enid, curling an arm around the woman's shoulders.

"Thank you, Carl," Swift went on, nodding at Sands. "PC Sands, call it in. We need a BOLO for a Jacob Mortimore." He turned his attention back to the Mortimores. "We need a brief description; age, height, hair colour, any distinguishing marks, where he was going."

Carl's face crumpled; Annie couldn't make out what he was saying.

"He was supposed to be away with Leon," the woman sitting comforting her friend said. She was slightly younger than the Mortimores, well-dressed with shiny hair and a pretty face. "He's eighteen, dark hair, green eyes. I'm sorry but I don't know what he was last wearing."

She turned to Enid who shook her head. "I can't remember. I can't remember." The words cut through Annie like a knife.

Swift gave Sands the nod and the young PC disappeared out of the stifling living room. Annie pulled at the scarf around her neck and laid it in her lap.

"Can you tell me your names?" Swift asked the couple yet to be introduced.

"Oh god, sorry, yes," the woman said, her round eyes huge. "I'm Sally, this is Edward, my husband. Brampton, Edward and Sally Brampton. I went to school with Enid. This is just awful. Leon and Jacob were supposed to be going away with a boy called Aaron too, but he had to pull out of the trip."

Swift looked at Annie. She nodded at him, and he pulled the bagged-up phone from his pocket.

"Does this belong to Jacob?" he asked, pressing the phone through the bag so it lit up.

Carl looked at the naked women on the screen and screwed his nose up through his tears. "They're good lads. That's not theirs."

Swift looked to Sally who shook her head, and he slid the phone away.

"Is Leon okay?" Sally asked, her bottom lip wobbling. "Could you ask him where Jacob is, maybe?"

As though this glimmer of hope had given Enid something to believe in, her face opened and she stared at the officers. Annie felt her stomach twist with the pain in the woman's eyes.

"He's not awake yet," Annie said, softly, bile rising in her throat as Enid sank back down into despair. "Doctors have put him in a medically induced coma so his body can heal. But as soon as he's able to, we will do everything we can to talk to him about where Jacob might be. And in the meantime, we'll do everything we can to find your boy."

The words felt hollow as she spoke them. But it's what people expect them to say. It's the hope that keeps family members and loved ones alive in times like these.

"We're a small town, detectives." The man sitting next to Swift on the sofa finally broke his silence. "Things like this can tear apart a whole community. We're all friends and we want to do anything we can to find Jacob. Can we start a search party, we need to be out there looking. I don't feel right sitting here doing nothing. Our son is friends with Leon and Jacob and I just can't imagine…"

Edward Brampton's unspoken words stumbled across the room as his face sagged.

"What can you tell us about the trip the boys had planned?" Annie asked, knowing the last thing Swift needed was a group of people out searching and potentially destroying a crime scene, and with it, clues to Jacob's whereabouts. "Where did they say they were going? Who with?"

Enid Mortimore sniffed, wiping her face with the

sleeve of her jumper. "It was a boys' trip, just a few nights away in a caravan park in Norfolk. Like Butlins but cheaper, you know? They're all taking exams next summer and they wanted to let off some steam. I… I wish I'd said no."

Tears streamed down her face and no matter how much she soaked them up with the knitted wool of her sleeve, they kept appearing. Sally Brampton wrapped her arm around Enid's shoulder and hugged her tightly.

"Was it just the three of them who decided to go? Leon, Jacob, and Aaron?" Swift asked.

Carl Mortimore nodded, his chins wobbling. "They're best friends, you know? Boys trip like my wife just said. Even if you had said no, love, Jacob would have gone anyway." He turned his attention back to Annie and Swift. "He always does what he wants, our Jacob. He's very sensible though. He's a good lad. He'll be okay, won't he?"

Neither Annie nor Swift gave a reply. It wasn't in their nature to lie to make things easier.

"Was there anything out of the ordinary about the boys in the lead-up to their trip?" Annie asked.

The parents looked at each other, Enid licked her lips, her gaze dropping back to her hands in her lap, her fingers twisted so hard the skin had gone pure white.

"Excitement, maybe?" Carl said. "They were all pretty boisterous. They're kind of past that age where Christmas is fun, so to see them all revved up was neat. It made a change from the sullen chumps they had been the past few months."

Annie nodded, a seed of thought planted in her brain. She didn't think too much about it, or what had caused it for fear it would vanish before it had percolated into something tangible. Annie's thoughts were like that, dreams she needed to leave alone. But given the state Leon had been in when he appeared out of the lake, Annie wasn't sure time was something Jacob had a lot of.

She turned to Sally Brampton. "You said your son is friends with Leon and Jacob." Sally nodded, her hug tightening around Enid's weary body. "Was he involved in the trip at all?"

"We said he could go if he could pay for it by himself," Edward replied. "But he's been a bit under the weather so when the others got a Saturday job together, he thought he could get away with staying at home instead of joining them. But we stood our ground when it came to paying for the trip."

The guilt written over Edward and Sally's faces that their own son was at home and safe, was as clear as if they'd harmed the other boys themselves.

"You weren't to know," Enid sniffed, picking up on it.

"So Aaron, Leon, and Jacob all work together?" Swift asked.

Carl took Enid's hands in his and nodded. "They're all helping out at the construction site a few towns over. Just Saturdays, but it's manual labour and they get paid a fair whack for it. Please, detectives, I know you're only doing your jobs here, but we need to get out there to look for our son."

Swift stood from the sofa. "We have teams assembling right now, Mr Mortimore. We will do our best to find your boy. PC Sands here needs your permission to search Jacob's room and we will need access to any electronics he was using."

"Anything," Enid said, silent tears still coating her cheeks. "Anything you need, just find our boy."

Annie pushed herself from the arm of the sofa and grabbed her scarf as it slid to the floor. She followed Swift out of the house and back into the frigid air. Outside on the green was a flurry of activity now. Blue lights flashed as backup arrived and they headed in the direction of the uniformed officers.

"Annie, I want to go and see Leon for myself," Swift said, after giving the officer in charge a run-down of what he knew. "Those boys were supposed to be enjoying a New Year trip away and this is how it's ended up. I just hope we're in time to find Jacob."

Annie felt the same. But if the boys had been missing for five days already, the chances of that being true were fading fast.

SIX

THE NURSES IN CHARGE OF LEON'S CARE WEREN'T too happy to see Annie and Swift. Normally the DI could sway people with a smile and a little bit of charm, but as soon as he flashed his badge and introduced them to the team, their shutters came down.

"He's far too ill to talk to anyone, let alone you." One of the charge nurses had said as soon as Swift had flipped open his wallet. She had led the two detectives around the ward, past Leon's private room, and into a family area that was hotter than Majorca had been last summer and smelt like cabbages.

"Remind me never to get so ill I end up in hospital," Swift said, pacing back and forth in the windowless room.

Annie cocked her head at him and sighed. "She's looking out for her patient, it's her job. If you ended up here you'd be lucky enough to get great care and…, will you stop walking about like a caged animal and sit down, you're making me nervous."

"Yeah well, hospitals make me nervous," he said, plonking himself down on the plastic-coated chair next to Annie.

She looked at him, his knee bouncing like a cricket's.

"You're not having anything done."

Swift shrugged. "They still scare me. Don't they scare you? Especially after…, you know?"

Annie's eyebrows shot into her hair. "Plague doctor or broken ankle?"

"All of the above." Swift waved his hands around. "All of the above and more."

"Is it pain you're scared of, or can you just not handle being in control?" The words had tumbled from Annie's lips before she had a chance to think about what she was saying.

Luckily, the scary nurse chose that moment to arrive back in the room. She stepped in and closed the door behind her, taking a seat opposite Annie and Swift. It squeaked as she sat down.

"Leon Scutts is incredibly poorly." She lifted a hand to Swift as he sat forward "Let me say what I've got to say first. Leon Scutts is incredibly poorly, but he's still alive. We need to keep him that way and having your lot here asking questions and prodding him this way and that isn't helping his cause."

"Sorry, Nurse?" Annie prompted, putting a calming hand on Swift's knee.

"Nurse Beche. Lauren Beche."

"Thank you, Nurse Beche," Annie went on. "We know that Leon is unwell and the last thing we want to do is make him any worse, but another boy is missing and we need to find him."

The blood drained from Nurse Beche's face. "What?"

Swift nodded. "We only just found out, we have teams out looking for him but we're still stumped as to where Leon was for the last five days, and if we knew that then we might have a better chance at finding Jacob Mortimore before anything happens to him."

"Right," Nurse Beche shifted in her seat, the material squeaking under her. "Okay, that's different. If this other boy was in the same predicament as Leon then I'd say he has a maximum of another few hours before he succumbs to whatever injuries it is they have."

"Are you able to tell us anything about Leon's injuries?" Annie asked. "What do you think caused them?"

Nurse Beche took a deep breath and stood up. Annie feared she was going to tell them to leave, that she was too busy to answer questions.

"Come with me," she said, instead, holding the family room door open for the detectives.

They followed the nurse along the corridor, the yellow paint designed to make it a brighter place to be just made Swift look jaundiced he was so pale. Their shoes squeaked on the polished floor, echoing around the surprisingly quiet ward.

Leon Scutts had a room to himself. He lay in the hospital bed, vulnerable in the middle of the room. Wires and tubes poked out from beneath the eponymous blue blanket, his eyes were taped shut but Annie could see how thin his lids were. The swelling and discolouration of the rest of his body were starting to calm, the blanket hid a thinner body beneath it, the arms by Leon's sides were a mottled pinky-blue now. His face was pale, still a stark difference from the colour of his torso.

The room was noisier than the corridor had been. Beeps and whirs from the machines keeping Leon alive filled the space. Annie walked up to the bed and placed a hand over Leon's. His skin was cool to touch but softer than she had imagined. She tucked his arm under the blanket and turned back to look at Swift and the nurse.

Nurse Beche was looking at the files at the bottom of Leon's bed, flicking the paper over to read the new entries onto his charts. Swift was standing in the doorway looking pale. Pulling a chair out from beside Leon's bed, Annie slid it quietly across the floor and gestured for Swift to sit down. He took it and slid into it, a grateful look on his face.

"His temperature is stable," the nurse said, placing the files back on the foot of the bed. "That's one good thing. When he arrived he was hypothermic, we had to wrap him in a heated body warmer to bring him back up to temp. But even then he couldn't hold it."

"What else can you tell us?" Swift asked, looking at Leon.

Nurse Beche moved around the hospital bed and looked at the detectives across Leon's prone body. She placed a gentle hand on the boy's forehead and stroked the hair from his eyes.

"His skin was so bloated it was stretched and sagging by the time he got here. Very much what we see in patients who've suffered drowning or immersion injuries. All except his face. It looked as though he'd been in the water up to his neck and stayed there. But, at this time of year and with these temperatures, I would have expected him to have been already dead. The human body can only withstand extreme cold temperatures for a matter of hours, a day maximum. It doesn't make any sense."

Annie thought back to the tepid water of the lake. "If the water was warmer, how long would a human survive submerged?"

"If their head was uncovered? A few days, maybe, depends on a number of other factors. Obviously, he'd need to be eating and drinking. And for someone to stay willingly under-water for that long is unheard of. So we'd be looking at other injuries that may cause submersion, which in themselves could be life-threatening."

"Does Leon have any other injuries?" Swift asked,

starting to look a better colour. "Other than the submersion bloating?"

"He was in renal failure when he arrived, but that could be down to the submersion. He's also in the early stages of septicaemia. We're lucky we caught that one, given the colour of his skin. That would have killed him in hours."

"Was that because of the water?" Annie asked.

"We're not sure," Nurse Beche went on. "It could be. Depends what kind of water he was in, and if he had any open wounds to speak of. There were no visible ones we could see but that doesn't mean he didn't have them to start with. He also had a broken femur."

"Wow, he's young for a broken femur," Annie interrupted, thinking of all the elderly people she'd seen in her training who'd broken their hips in a fall.

"Was this pre or post submersion?" Swift added.

One of the machines next to Leon started to sound out an alarm. Annie felt the skin on her scalp shrink with the high-pitched beeping. The nurse didn't look worried, Annie took this as a good sign, the same way she looked to the flight attendants during turbulence.

"We're not sure. It looked recent," Nurse Beche said, unhooking a bag from the drip stand and pulling the tube from one of Leon's cannulas. "It could have been the reason he was submerged for such a long time. A broken thigh bone is painful and debilitating. If it happened to him when he fell into the body of water, then it could have stopped him climbing out?"

She took a new bag from the tray by Leon's bed and attached it back to his arm and the IV stand. She stood squeezing it for a while until the alarm discontinued and plunged the room back into a cacophony of beeps and whirs instead.

"Any idea how such an injury could have happened?" Annie asked.

"Your guess is as good as mine, detective," the nurse replied, going back to stroking Leon's hair. "Normally an injury like that would bruise quite significantly, but the colouration of his skin at the time of admission meant that we couldn't see any bruises or the like."

"And no signs of head wounds or injuries on the parts you could see?" Swift asked.

"Nothing, no," Nurse Beche replied. "He looked to be well nourished, his hair and teeth in great condition. We had no concerns around his health apart from the broken leg and the… well the obvious."

Swift nodded. "Thank you."

"If you don't mind, I'll need to be getting on with rounds," said the nurse. "Can I trust you to not try anything stupid if I leave you here?"

Annie nodded, nudging Swift with her toe because he was too engrossed in looking at Leon's face to reply.

"What? Oh yes, sorry. Of course. I promise to keep my distance and only talk to him if he talks to me first." Swift held up his hands and grimaced. "Sorry, we really do appreciate what you're doing."

The nurse opened the door and stepped out. "I hope you find that other boy, detectives."

She disappeared without waiting for a reply.

"You and me both," Swift said, getting off his chair and leaning over Leon.

Annie watched him work. The way he moved his eyes down over the boy's face, his neck and chest. He stayed by his word and didn't touch Leon or try to talk to him.

"What are you thinking?" Annie asked as Swift lowered himself back into his chair.

"So, we're thinking the swelling is from submersion, yes?"

Annie nodded.

"And Leon had a broken leg. Maybe the boys were in an accident and ended up in the lake? Somehow Leon stayed above the water and managed to free himself by walking out five days later even though he was in pain and probably should have walked out when the accident happened…"

"Yeah," Annie agreed with Swift's crumpled brow. "How does that make any sense?"

"All we know for sure is that Leon was in water for up to five days, most likely the lake given his temperature and the fact he made it out alive."

"What we need to know is how and why." Annie scratched the back of her neck. "Do you know if the bloods showed up any other traces of alcohol or drugs in Leon's blood? Didn't Robins say something about Codeine? That makes even less sense."

"No other drugs, no," said Swift as he tapped his fingers on his knee. "But I'm not sure about alcohol. We need to find Tink and Page to see if they know. I think we might have pushed our luck enough with Nurse Beche."

As it happened, Tink and Page found Annie and Swift as they were leaving the hospital ward. Page was running so fast he nearly battle rammed into Annie and it was only the quick thinking of Swift as he grabbed her elbow that kept her upright.

"Has no one ever told you it's dangerous to run in corridors, especially ones where you might bump into elderly people or the injured? Quite literally."

Annie lifted herself out of Swift's arms and gave him a look. "I'll have you know I'm neither."

Swift flushed. "Well yes, I obviously didn't mean you. That's not what I meant at all. Just that…"

"I'm pulling your leg," Annie interrupted, grinning at the DI, before turning to Tink and Page. "What are you guys in such a hurry for anyway?"

Page looked distraught; his face drawn. "It's Jacob Mortimore. He's been found."

Swift straightened himself and brushed down his coat. "Has he been admitted yet? Still in A&E? Is he talking?"

Annie looked between the two young officers, a horrible sense of realisation washing over her. "He didn't make it, did he?"

Tink shook her head. "He's being taken down to Evans as we speak."

SEVEN

Swift and Annie made it to the mortuary before Jacob's body did. They waited for Evans in the foyer; Annie drew her coat around herself and burrowed her chin into her scarf. It wasn't that the mortuary was any colder than normal, it was that the coldness had seeped into her bones in Lowan and was lying there like an unwanted visitor.

She couldn't imagine how cold Leon must have felt, naked and soaked through on the shore of Lowanford Lake in the middle of a December night, but she hoped he had already been out of it enough to not feel it. And, as for Jacob, Annie hoped he hadn't suffered at all.

"Evening detectives." Evans' voice carried across the corridor. "Nice to see you both. It's been a while."

"You too, Evans," Annie said, putting a hand on the man's white-coated arm. "How's the family?"

Evans ran a hand through his pink hair, his eyes

darting to the PVC strip curtain between his office and the morgue.

"Keeping well, thanks, Annie. Thankfully. How about you guys? How's Mim?" Evans led them through to his desk and gestured for them to take a seat.

Evans and his husband were in the process of fostering their second child but at times like these Annie couldn't imagine having children of her own when the fragility of life was so apparent around her. She found it hard enough imagining Sunday back out alone and in the cold, and he was just a cat.

Shaking her head she focused on the task at hand and not the *what-ifs* that she had no control over. Sunday had been quite peacefully sleeping next to his favourite pot plant when Annie had left her flat that morning. He was safe. Swift was safe. Mim was away working and her torrent of texts let Annie know that she was safe too.

"Crazy as ever," Annie replied to Evans. "She's in sunny Scotland at the moment working on the designs for some artsy festival or other. Drawing things. I think. I'm still not one hundred percent sure what it is she does for a living but from the photos she Whataspped me last night, she's having a ball."

"Splendid," Evans said, booting up his computer.

Swift looked at Annie with a furrowed brow. Annie mouthed back at him, *what?* But Swift shook his head as Evans cleared his throat, a sombre look falling over his face.

"Do you want to watch the autopsy?" he asked. "It's late, but I'm going to start it now as I've got a batch of work arriving tomorrow from a hospital in the next county. Their pathologist is awol and they've resorted to shipping their dead to me. Not like I don't have enough work of my… sorry, sorry, mustn't moan."

"You can moan if you need to, Evans," said Annie. "We're a safe space to moan in."

Evans ran another hand through his hair and Annie noticed the sag to his skin, the tiredness in his eyes. So much for New Year new them. Working in this industry meant there was no rest for anyone, not anytime.

"I think we should," Swift replied to Evans. "If you're okay with that, O'Malley?"

Was she?

Annie had seen dead bodies before; she'd spoken to Evans about the results of his work. She'd even seen the bodies after he'd finished. But she'd never sat through the process because she'd already dropped out of police training before that joy came around.

"I won't know unless I try," she said, truthfully.

"I'll go and set up, give me fifteen minutes." Evans tapped away quickly on his keyboard, studying the screen, and then stood and headed through the plastic curtains to the mortuary.

"Is Mim really in Scotland?" Swift asked when Evans had gone.

"Yeah, she left a couple of days ago. Why?"

"Oh, no reason."

The room descended into silence. Annie pondered over Swift's question until her brain was as wound up as a ball of wool. Why did Swift care where Mim was? What was going on with Swift?

"Urgh," she said, dropping her head into her hands at the idea something was going on between her sister and Swift.

Mim had been the one to nudge Annie to tell Swift how she felt about him, so there was no way she'd go behind her back. Is there?

"You alright there, O'Malley?"

Annie looked over at Swift whose face had blossomed into a grin.

"Tiptop," she muttered into her fingers.

"Okay," he replied, still looking at her curiously. "We should go through. If you need to leave at any point, please do."

"Trying to get rid of me, Swift?" Annie asked, not waiting for an answer.

She pushed through the plastic flaps and the smell hit her like a freight train. Decomposition. Death. The smell of a butcher's shop with added metal and, weirdly, rotting fish. Her hand flew automatically to cover her mouth and nose but that did little to block the putrid smell.

"Jeez," she said, her voice muffled.

Swift put a steady arm on her shoulder. "You okay?"

Annie nodded, her eyes watering.

"Yep, sorry guys, Jacob's body is pretty fresh, there's some Vicks on the side if you need it." Evans stood beside the fixed gurney in the middle of the room. Jacob's body was laid out ready.

Intrigue overcame Annie's initial feelings as she stepped up towards Jacob and looked over what he had become. With her eyes fixed on the gurney, Annie dabbed her finger in the Vicks and rubbed it under her nose. Offering it to Swift, Annie's focus was entirely on the body laid out in front of them now.

"He's not blue," she said, looking up at Evans.

Evans shook his head and started to methodically go through Jacob's hair with tweezers then a comb, brushing out and collecting samples of foreign bodies and detritus. "He has a very different look to your other boy. I haven't seen him to work on, obviously, he's still alive. But from what I hear, Leon was bloated as though he'd been submerged for a few days, yes?"

Swift nodded in agreement. "Bloated and blue."

"Jacob has been in water, you can see from his fingers," Evans continued, holding up the boy's hand and spreading his fingers out. Annie moved closer, spotting the tell-tale wrinkles in the tips of Jacob's fingers. Swimmers' hands, or the hands of someone who'd stayed in the bath too long. "But he wasn't submerged for long because his skin isn't bloated and hasn't taken on a lot of the water itself. He's also got the normal colouration of someone *not* submerged in water for a length of time. No large open wounds etc

etc. I'd say your boy was in the water for less than a couple of hours, four or five maximum."

"Where was his body found?" Swift asked.

"By the lake, same spot where Leon emerged," Evans replied.

Annie and Swift looked across at each other. They'd been there that morning and had seen no sign of Jacob or anyone else for that matter. But they hadn't gone in the water, and they hadn't really looked at the surface of the lake. If they had, would Jacob still be alive? If they'd let his parents go and search, would Jacob be in the hospital with his friend and not lying on the cold mortuary table in front of them now?

"How long has he been dead?" Annie asked.

Evans studied the paperwork that had arrived with Jacob's body. "Temperature would suggest about three hours. But given the temperature of the water of the lake and the air around it, I'll do some more tests to determine. If you look though, liver mortis has started to set in and we're at the very early stages of rigor. So my guess is anywhere between 2 and four hours."

Annie felt her stomach churn. "So he was still alive when we were in Lowen this morning?"

"Yes, he would have been alive," Evans went on, not helping matters. "But, who knows how well he would have been or if finding him this morning would have made a difference, Annie."

"What do you mean?" Swift asked.

Evans put down the comb and looked across at the detectives. "If you look at both of his arms, and even his feet, you'll see the start of tissue necrosis and abscess at a number of sites."

"Intravenous drugs?" Annie asked.

"I won't know until we've got tox results back, but it looks like it to me." Evans lifted Jacob's arm again and twisted it gently outwards.

Annie looked at where Evans' gloved finger was pointing. Through the whiteness of Jacob's skin, there was a purple blister at the crook of his elbow. The centre of the blister was a single circle of what looked like the mould that sometimes gathered on the tops of the mugs left in the office over the weekend.

"Oh." Annie took a step back, feeling her head swim.

"What's happening here?" Swift asked, stepping closer to Annie, and slipping an arm across her back.

"Tissue necrosis," Evans replied, swabbing the wound, and bagging the swab. "Normally reserved for those who inject with dirty needles or who get infections at the site of entry."

"Jacob was using drugs?" Annie asked, leaning into Swift's arm.

"I won't be able to answer that until the tox results are back."

"Is there anything else you can tell us at the moment?" said Swift. "Cause of death? Any other injuries?"

Evans looked over Jacob's body again, taking in

each minute detail with precision. He scraped under the boy's fingernails and looked under his eyelids and in his mouth. Annie and Swift watched in silence as he turned the boy over as carefully as he could and shone the light over the back of Jacob's body. Liver mortis had started to turn the boy's skin black as blood pooled, unable to be pumped around his body since the last beat of his heart. Half an hour passed as Evans worked his way over Jacob looking for clues as to how he had ended up dead on the shore of Lowenford Lake.

He put down the small tweezers he held in his hand and looked up at the detectives.

"There are no outward signs of cause of death and until I get bloods and tox back, and until I open him up, I can't tell you what killed him." Evans pulled off his gloves and put them in the yellow waste bin. "I can tell you that he has what feels like a broken right humerus and the infection I showed you in the right hand cephalic intermediate vein is found also in the veins of the left hand and the dorsal venous arch of bilateral feet."

"English, Evans," Annie asked.

"Sorry, the injection sites in both elbows and both feet are infected."

Swift whistled through his teeth. "Thanks, Evans, we won't stay for the next part, but can you call me if anything rings alarm bells when you do open him up?"

Evans nodded. "I'll be sure to do that, Swift. And

Annie, I saw that look on your face when you heard how long he had been dead. Please don't put yourself in the position of *what-ifs*. It'll hurt more than it helps. You and Swift are the good guys, you didn't put Jacob in the water, you didn't hurt either him or Leon, so you remember that, hey love?"

Annie nodded, her empty stomach swirling with acidic guilt. She may not have hurt them but if Evans' timings were right then Jacob may very well have been in the lake as Annie and Swift walked by. And if she hadn't been so fixated on the other things on her mind, there was a small chance that Jacob could still be alive.

EIGHT

TUESDAY

Annie hadn't slept a wink. She'd tossed and turned and when she did eventually fall into a broken fit of sleep, her dreams were vivid with images of Jacob and Leon reaching out to her from the lake. She'd tried to save them, she'd reached back and tried to grip at their hands, but they'd been too slippery and she'd not been able to keep hold. One by one they'd descended into the black water and Annie had woken with a start and a deep sense of dread.

She looked at her bedside clock and even though it only read four thirty, Annie knew she wasn't going back to sleep. Sliding quietly from the camp bed so as not to wake Sunday, Annie crept up to the tiny bathroom at the top of the building and showered herself awake. Only thirty minutes later, she was swiping her card into the staff entrance of the station with a home-made coffee cradled in her hands.

Outside the rain was hammering down, the sound of fingers tapping on glass followed Annie through the corridors making her feel more chilled than necessary in a place she knew kept her safe. Shrugging out of her soaking wet jacket, Annie hung it on the coat hooks at the back of the room rather than over her chair as she normally did, not fancying sitting in a puddle of water while she got to work.

Not work work, but rather a secret kind of mission she'd set herself for the new year, one Annie wasn't really admitting to herself yet, either. She booted up her computer and warmed her hands around her mug while it whirred to life. The rest of the station was dead, which was perfect for what Annie was about to do, but less than perfect for her nerves. Though used to being alone, Annie liked the sounds outside her city centre flat; the sound of revellers out enjoying the pubs, the early morning deliveries to the restaurants and shops along her road. She lived above a pizza place that always made her feel hungry because Pete the Pizzaman's food was what had kept her sustained and happy for as long as Annie had lived there. She made a mental note to go and see him later that evening, maybe she'd get a takeout and deliver it to Swift, she had some party bits and bobs to drop off at his house anyway.

The screen flashed to life and Annie took a deep

breath and logged in. She navigated through the ancient system to find the staff files and typed in her mum's name. Growing up, Annie thought she knew all there was to know about her parents. That her mum was overprotective, angsty, scared, and angry at the same time because she was always on high alert that her husband would come back and take his other daughter. To Annie, she was a school cook who had done her best in a difficult situation.

But ever since Annie had found Mim her whole past had unravelled like a badly knitted scarf mauled by Sunday the cat. Both their parents were police officers, and while her dad was well-known and decorated, her mum worked undercover in vice. Pretty much as far away from a meek school cook as she could get. According to Mim, their dad had fled because he was scared. Annie needed to find out what he was scared of and what had happened to her mum to make her kill a man. Who was he? Why did she do it? And, probably the most important question of all, the question Annie knew she wasn't going to find hidden in the depths of the station archives, why hadn't she told her daughter the truth?

The search engine on the system was as old as the system itself and most of the files Annie had found were scanned copies from paper, which meant it took a few tries to find the right person. As the list of names on Annie's search grew smaller, the sun had started to rise, casting rays through the windows and warming the patches of carpet it landed on. Annie blinked and stretched, her shoulders and neck aching. It was already nearly six and the teams would start to arrive in the next hour, especially her own team given the case they were working on.

A link to her mum's name was staring at her from the screen. A little Pandora's box. Annie got up and walked around in a circle, tapping her fingers against her lips.

Come on, O'Malley. Come on.

Dropping back to her seat, Annie moved her mouse over the link, closed her eyes, and clicked. The door to the office opened and Annie swivelled in her chair to see who it was.

Swift, crap.

Annie flicked her screen off the search results and tried not to scream at the awful timing of her boss.

"Oh, Annie, you're early," Swift said, faltering at the door. He was holding something in his hand which was quickly moved out of sight behind him.

"Yeah, you know?" she said, wracking her brains for a good enough reason to be in before she had to. "I wanted to get a start on the… thing."

"Me too," Swift said. "The… thing. That's it."

He took off his coat and hid whatever it was underneath it on the hook before coming to take a seat next to Annie.

"What thing is that?" he asked, nodding at Annie's screen.

In her haste to hide her real reason for being in, Annie had flicked across to her emails and, right there in full view of probably the whole of Norwich, was a gift from Rose in the form of a half-naked man holding a banner with the words *here's to finding me in 2024* written across is.

Annie's face flushed the same colour as the party hat the man was wearing.

"Sorry, I'll tell Rose not to email inappropriate things to me at work," Annie muttered, hitting delete.

Swift laughed. "No wonder you're so happy about your resolutions if that's one of them."

"Oh no, it's not. He's not. Definitely not one of my resolutions." Annie wished the ground would swallow her up.

"Well he should be," Swift said, turning on his computer. "You deserve a great year."

"Right, thanks." Annie didn't want a great year with a six-pack and a banner, but she wasn't about to tell Swift that.

"Let's go and warm up the incident room," he continued. "We can regroup when Tink and Page get here and figure out what we have."

As Swift made his way out of the office, Annie flicked her screen back to the search results and almost shouted out in despair as she read the word RESTRICTED in red letters.

Thumping the desk, she ran after him and they made their way down the corridor through the double doors to the incident room Tink had set up the previous day.

"Do you know how Leon is doing?" Annie asked, clearing her mind and squeezing past Swift as he held the door open for her.

"Not yet," he replied, flicking on the lights and putting his folders down on the centre table. "I'm hoping Page will have an update."

"Page does have an update," the young DC said coming through the door with a smile on his face and a tray of Starbucks in his hands, a carrier bag dangling from his finger. "Let's get these down us and I'll share what I found out about the boy yesterday. Tink must be on her way too, I saw the Tinkmobile in the carpark."

"She is indeed," Tink said, poking her head around the wide shoulders of Page. "Morning campers, you're all as eager as each other today."

It was still before seven, but the MCU team was settled and full of coffee and pastries and ready to get on with finding out what happened to Jacob and Leon. Tink had prepared the whiteboard with a photo of Leon, before and after. She added a picture of Jacob and pulled the lid from a marker to start writing as Page took to his feet.

"Page," said Swift, wiping crumbs from the table. "You were tasked with finding out about Leon, what can you tell us?"

"Thanks, Swift." Page stood next to Tink by the whiteboard and took out his notepad. "Leon Scutts, eighteen, student at the local high school about to do his A Levels. By all accounts he's conscientious, kind, and he never gets into trouble."

"And by other accounts?" Annie asked, knowing that parents and friends were less likely to talk ill of people who were dead or who'd nearly died.

"Well, I did some digging, and I couldn't find *anything* on him. Nothing. No high jinks, no animosity between him and his younger brothers— and I bribed them with the new PlayStation release too, his teachers had only good things to say. His social media was nothing to write home about and the tech guys are still going through his computer and they've said it's normal teen stuff."

"What about his phone?" Swift asked.

"No sign of it," Page replied. "And if it had been in the water with him then it's long gone."

"So there is nothing at all to give any clues as to where he had been and why he was the way he was when he reappeared?"

"Nope, the only thing that rang bells was the caravan park where the boys were supposed to be staying."

"Which was?" Swift prompted.

"That there was never any record of a booking by them. In fact, the park is shut over the winter."

Tink wrote this in capital letters on the whiteboard and Annie sat forward. "Meaning they were never planning to go on holiday together? Or they were planning something else, somewhere else?"

"We're not sure yet, tech haven't found anything on Leon's computer for a trip anywhere, but it might not have been him who organised it."

"Speaking of which," Swift said, tapping his pen against his lips. "We need to look into Jacob and see what role he had in all this."

"Way ahead of you, Swift," Page said, beaming for a millisecond then dropping his smile to a more appropriate sombre look. "Sorry, it's just been great to have been given more responsibility."

"You won't be saying that when you're DI." Swift winked at him. "What have you found out about Jacob?"

"Tech are on it with his electricals too," Page started, flicking the page on his pad. "But the school has said his family have been struggling financially this year, last year, this year? Sorry, I'm confused about school years. But anyway, they said Jacob was a great student but had struggled more with his studies this year as he was working so hard outside of school too."

"Good enough reason to *not* go away on holiday, surely?" Tink asked, jotting notes on the whiteboard.

"Maybe his parents wanted him to have a break so he could come back after the holidays feeling refreshed?" Annie said, feeling sick at the thought that Jacob would never be going back to school, would never be feeling refreshed.

"But if his parents cared that much about his

schooling then why let him work every spare hour he had at the building site?"

Annie's senses tingled. "Building site? Jacob's mum said yesterday they worked together at a site over in the next village."

"Yeah, the boys went to the same school and were great friends, so much so they worked together," Page said, running a finger down his pad as he searched. "Yep, here we go. They both worked for Kirkpatrick Constructions. Leon at the weekends and Jacob whenever he had a free day or hour by the looks of it."

"Kirkpatrick?" Swift stood slowly from his seat and walked around to Page, angling the DC's wrist so that he could see the writing on his pad. "Why does that name ring a bell?"

"Cameron Kirkpatrick," Annie answered, her mind whirring. "Local developer, turned up at the lake not long after officers did yesterday morning, seems to know a lot about the people who live in Lowan."

Tink drew his name in large letters on the board and circled it in red pen.

"You think he's got something to do with our boys?" she asked the room.

"I think his name has popped up more than it should have done if his presence was a coincidence," Swift said. "Tink, do you have anything to add about Leon's past medical history before we head out?"

Tink shook her head. "Nothing out of the ordinary. In great health as far as his doctors were allowed

74

to tell me. Hospital records show no admission since birth. Dead ends here, Swift."

"Right, in which case, can you two go and chase Evans for tox and blood results?" Swift indicated Tink and Page before turning his attention to Annie. "O'Malley, we're going to pay Mr Cameron Kirkpatrick a visit."

NINE

CAMERON KIRKPATRICK WAS A MAN ON A MISSION. HE
greeted Annie and Swift at the door to his office
building in the middle of the city and hadn't stopped
moving since they introduced themselves. It was no
wonder the man looked like he spent hours pumping
iron in the gym, he probably needed to build his
strength up if he was like this every day. With immac-
ulately preened blonde hair and a suit that was definitely not off the rack, Annie felt like the real
Cameron Kirkpatrick was hiding under a glossy
exterior.

"It's always go go go here at Kirkpatrick
Constructions," Cameron said, looking back over his
shoulder at the detectives.

They had whizzed along the marble corridors
where pictures of houses and office blocks had been
blown up to giant proportions and hung on the walls
and were now climbing the stairs to what felt like the

top floor. Annie was sure she'd seen the doors of a lift back in the reception but had no breath left in her body to mutter her thoughts to Swift. Besides, the DI looked one more flight short of a heart attack himself. Annie steeled herself as they rounded the top of the stairs, ready to tackle more, when Cameron pushed open the doors to an office that would have given Google headquarters a run for its money.

It was open plan, very different from the one where Annie and Swift rolled up to every morning. Pool tables lined the centre, brightly coloured pictures filled the walls, around the edge were tables with 3D models of what Annie assumed were some of the Kirkpatrick Constructions designs. It was a happy space filled with what looked like a handful of happy workers.

"It's like a construction version of the Micky Mouse Funhouse," Swift muttered beside her.

"Well then, detectives, here is my sanctuary," Cameron said, interrupting Annie's reply. "Please, let's sit."

They followed Cameron to a cluster of bright orange sofas in the far corner of the room and he gestured for them to take a seat. Annie dropped onto the sofa and tried not to make it obvious it was the comfiest sofa she'd ever sat on. Or maybe that was the five flights of stairs talking.

"Can I get you guys a drink? Green tea? Matcha? Boba tea?"

"Coffee, black." Apparently Swift wasn't in the mood for niceties.

Annie stopped herself from ordering a Mango Colada with whipped cream and settled for a cup of tea. Cameron clicked his fingers and a young man, no older than the boys they were there to talk about, appeared almost out of thin air. With their orders given, Cameron sank onto the sofa opposite Swift and Annie and steepled his fingers.

"I guess you're here to talk about those poor boys?"

Annie had a sudden urge to slap the insincere look from Cameron's face.

"Boys?" Swift said. "I heard from our officers that you were on the scene not long after they arrived at Lowanford Lake to look into what occurred with Leon, the boy who walked out of the water on New Year's Eve. What makes you say boys, plural?"

Cameron's wide eyes and sad mouth were like a bad performance at a primary school nativity. "I trust you know that a boy, Jacob Mortimore, was found dead there, too?"

"Of course *we* know," Swift shouted. "What I want to know is how *you* know. And why?"

If Cameron Kirkpatrick was shocked at Swift's outburst, he didn't show it. He looked around at the large room, eyes narrowed.

"Would you rather go somewhere more private, Mr Kirkpatrick?" Annie asked. "Your office, maybe?"

He smiled at her, turning her stomach. "This is my

office, sweetheart. I own the whole building and this floor is just for me. The others like coming here to hang out when they have free time. I should stop them, really, give myself a bit of privacy, you know? But I like the company."

His smile widened and Annie forced herself not to look away. Kirkpatrick Constructions were obviously doing well for themselves if he owned the whole building. It was prime real estate in the city centre.

"Would you like me to repeat my question, then?" Swift asked. "How do you know about what's happened and why?"

Cameron relaxed back in his seat, crossing his legs at the ankles and revealing socks that perfectly matched the decor.

"I am currently working with the council to secure some land in Lowan," he said, smiling. "I think I'm within my rights to keep abreast with the comings and goings in the town. Besides, both Leon and Jacob worked for me, on and off doing a little casual labour. I like to make sure my staff are okay, is that a crime? Or would you like to cuff me now, detective?"

He held his hands out to Annie and gave her a wink.

"You haven't answered DI Swift's question," she said, stony-faced. "You may think you have good enough reason to know *what's* going on, though I would question that, that doesn't tell us *how* you know, or how you knew so soon after it happened."

"My my, aren't you clever?" he said, smile slipping ever so slightly. "Or are you just trying to look good in front of your boss?"

Swift got out of his seat and stood over Cameron. "You can either answer here, or we can take you in. Do *you* want to look good in front of your *staff*, Mr Kirkpatrick, because trust me if I have to take you in, I'm not going to be doing it quietly."

"Oh, for goodness' sake, DI Swift, sit down." Cameron looked as calm as he had when they'd first arrived. Annie didn't like it, she felt wrong-footed. "Look, here come our drinks."

The young boy from earlier appeared with a tray of drinks. Setting it down on the coffee table he whispered into Cameron's ear before disappearing as quietly as he arrived. Two red spots grew on Cameron's cheeks and his mouth was set in a thin line; his demeanour had flipped one eighty degrees.

"Everything okay, Mr Kirkpatrick?" Annie asked, sipping at her tea.

"I'll tell you what's not alright, and it's not me caring about what goes on in Lowan," Cameron said, his voice a few octaves lower than it had been. "That busybody Windsor and his pathetic attempt to stop me moving my project forward. Why don't you do some proper work and find out why he's forcing me to put a pause on my entire year's work every five seconds because he's found another bloody clause that I have to fight? And I will fight, mark my words. Doesn't he want jobs and a bit of money injected into that shabby little backwater town he calls home?"

Swift shifted in his chair, his coffee left on the tray. "What is your plan for Lowan?"

"To make it a community," Cameron replied, focussing on Swift, his face shifting back to happy as though he'd just remembered why they were there.

"I'd say they're a pretty tight-knit community already," Annie added.

"Well, I think another few houses, a surgery, and a community centre will liven the place up a bit."

"And where are you planning on building this *community?*" she asked, picturing a soulless new build estate on the outskirts of Lowan, forcing it outwards with neither the roads nor the infrastructure to cope.

"Around the lake." Cameron eyed Annie.

"Around the lake?" That was a surprise.

"Yes," he hissed. "Around the bloody lake. There's nothing there now anyway except that weirdo's hut and fishermen who always look like they're freezing anyway. I've offered them good money."

"There's not a lot of space around the lake though," Swift interjected.

"Oh for god's sake, okay," Cameron looked riled now, his calm exterior too much hassle to keep on show. He stood, turned to the staff members halfway through a game of pool, and shouted at them. "You lot, get out."

For a man so keen to show the fun side of

working for Kirkpatrick Construction, the workers fled before Cameron had sat back down.

"I want that lake gone," he said when the room had emptied. "It's no secret, you'll find out soon enough. But my plans can't happen if that lake is still there. Three hundred houses won't build themselves, you know."

Three hundred? No wonder Windsor and his love of the history of Lowan was so keen to put a halt to the building work.

"And you're telling us you're doing this out of the goodness of your heart and the want to provide for the people of Lowan?" Annie scoffed.

Swift raised a hand. "I think we've heard enough for now." He stood up and Annie followed suit, the tea leaving a bitter aftertaste in her mouth. "Just one more thing, Mr Kirkpatrick, did you see or hear anything odd when you arrived at the lake yesterday morning?"

Cameron stood again, his arms crossed, shoulders slouched. He'd dropped his guard. Annie had seen Swift use this trick before, let them believe that they were off the record, a quick chat before the detectives left them to it. It was the time when truths came out and secrets were spilled because those who were keeping them were so relieved to have gotten away with it.

"Odd, the whole bloody place is odd." He smirked. "Windsor and his notebook follow me around every single time I set foot there. That old dude in the woods smells like weed. A lake that's oddly warm and supposedly magical? Imagine fishing in *that*. Give me strength. The sooner I get rid of that lake the better. Do you know what's actually making the water glow? Let me tell you. It's algae. Not magic, not healing properties, not fairies dancing around sprinkling everything with bloody fairy dust. No, it's a stinking great plant. So when Aaron called me to say Leon had come stumbling out of it like some kind of monster, it cemented the need to get the damn thing filled in. If the people of Lowan can't see that, then it's just on me to keep them safe."

Swift's phone cut through Kirkpatrick's tirade just in time to stop Annie from kicking the developer in the shins. He drew it out of his pocket and barked his name as he answered.

"Thank you for your time, Mr Kirkpatrick. We'll be in touch," Annie said, shaking Cameron's hand, her skin crawling.

Swift was hitting the buttons to call the lift as Cameron shut the door behind Annie, almost catching her on the backside.

"Thanks, Tink," he said, ending the call. "We'll see you in Lowan, on our way there now."

The lift doors pinged open and they stepped inside, soft muzak and the rich scent of tuberose greeting them.

"That was the others," Swift said, letting Annie go first. He pressed the button for the ground floor and waited for the doors to shut before he continued. "No signs of water on Jacob's lungs, he had hypothermia and signs of dehydration, but cause of death is being recorded as septicaemia."

"Blood poisoning?" Annie interjected. "Do they know what from?"

"The sites Evans showed us," Swift said as the lift started to slow. "On the inside of his elbows and his feet."

"The injection sites?"

"Yep." The doors opened and they walked out, signing out of the building in record time.

"Jacob was using intravenous drugs and that's what killed him?" Annie asked as they made their way back out to the car park.

"Infection from an injection site killed him," Swift said. "Evans is still waiting on the tox results to see what drug it was Jacob was injecting."

"It's a bit of a coincidence that two boys go missing from the same town, one dead, one almost dead, both from very different causes, for them not to be related, isn't it?" Annie added wondering why Leon's bloods had shown up clear of drugs and his best friend had died from them.

"It's not a coincidence," Swift said, unlocking his car. "They have to be related. The boys were away together, lied to their parents, they both turned up near the lake. Did you hear what Kirkpatrick let slip there?"

Annie nodded. "That it was Aaron who told him

about Leon. Why did Aaron call Cameron Kirkpatrick as soon as he regained consciousness?"

"I don't know, but it's got to be connected. Buckle up Annie, we need to get the lights on."

Swift's car didn't have lights, Annie had been in it enough times to know that. She had also been a passenger of his enough times to know he would drive like his car was flashing the blues and twos whether or not other drivers could see or hear them. She clicked her belt into place and grabbed hold of the handle above her head.

"What's happened?" she asked. "Why are we racing back to Lowan?"

Swift pulled out into the busy streets of the city centre and put his foot down. "It's Aaron, he's missing."

TEN

THE PLAYING FIELD WAS AWASH WITH POLICE CARS BY the time Annie and Swift arrived back in Lowan. A small unit command had been erected by one of the goal posts and a cold-looking uniformed officer was holding fort over a gathering crowd. Through the hat covered heads, Annie spotted Tink's bright blonde hair and Page who was standing a full head and shoulders above everyone else.

Swift pulled in behind Tink's car and they marched over the muddy playing field to their team.

"What can you tell us?" Swift asked Tink, a hand on her shoulder.

Tink looked concerned, her normally open face pinched and drawn. "Officers are searching his house now, and looking at his socials. Aaron's Mum, a Hannah Cooper, called it in about an hour ago, said she hadn't seen Aaron since yesterday and that's unusual."

"Yesterday?" Annie asked, feeling the cold pinch at her nose. "Why wait until today to call us, given what's been going on?"

"Aaron is a teenager who doesn't get out of bed when he doesn't have to," Tink replied. "They're on school holidays and it was only when Aaron's mum ventured into his room to see if he wanted anything to eat or drink that she realised he wasn't there."

"And how does she know he hasn't just gone out? When did she last see him yesterday?" Swift moved his team away from the crowd of locals who were starting to outnumber the uniformed officers. They stopped behind the row of police cars, out of earshot.

"Last night," Tink said, consulting her notepad. "Hannah said goodnight to him as normal and then went to bed. She said it was about half ten, which was early for Aaron but he'd been told to get rest by the doctors when he was in hospital and his mum said he'd been quiet and a bit subdued."

"Because he was the one who found Leon?" Annie asked.

"Because Leon found him," Page replied. "Aaron and his twin sister, Maisie, were by the lake when Leon reappeared. They weren't looking for him, just in the wrong place at the wrong time."

"But Aaron and Leon know each other?" Swift chewed at his bottom lip. "In fact, Aaron, Leon, and Jacob all knew each other."

"And they all worked for Kirkpatrick," Annie added.

Tink raised an eyebrow at her. "Aaron's mum and his twin sister, Maisie, are joining the search party, sorry Swift."

It was their policy to try and keep families from joining in with searching for loved ones. There was too much invested in it for them, too much emotion. And if the outcome wasn't good, they would forever have an image etched in their minds of their loved one's final moments. Swift also drummed it into his team about the importance of protecting a crime scene, and that was impossible to do when it's being trampled over by someone being ruled by their heart. Annie thought that came from Swift's harder side, but she understood the importance all the same. If locals wanted to search there was nothing they could do to stop it, so they joined in and took control

"Where are they?" he asked, eyes scanning the crowd over the top of the cars.

Tink spun around, taking a moment to find them before pointing a finger in the direction of a woman and young girl who would be easy to find even without Tink's guidance. The hollows of their eyes gave way to a horror that Annie knew well. It was the same look her mum had for at least a year after her dad had taken Annie's sister. They were standing with Carl Mortimore, Jacob's dad, and the husband of the couple who'd been at their house to help, Edward Brampton. Annie recognised the steely look on their faces and remembered the way Edward Brampton had wanted to start searching for Jacob when they were sitting in the Mortimore's living room. It was too late for Jacob, but despite his own loss, Jacob's dad was there helping to look for Aaron.

"Is it just the two of them?" Swift asked.

"Yep, three normally, with Aaron. Dad hasn't been around since their birth," Page replied. "Hannah works every hour to make ends meet. Must be hard with two teens; I know when I was growing up, I'd be constantly eating and still hungry. I can't imagine how families afford to feed kids these days, with prices so high for literally everything."

"These days?" Annie asked, brow raised. "You're barely out of school, Tom. Spare a thought for those of us over thirty."

Page smiled. "You don't look a day over twenty-nine, O'Malley."

Swift snorted and turned back from the crowd to his team. "Right, Tink and Page can you go and help with the search? Talk to people while you're out there, see if you can get some more info on these three boys. There's something that ties this group of lads together that their parents don't know about, and we need to find out what it is before someone else dies. Any parent in their right mind would spill their kids' secrets to make sure they're safe. We know people talk when they think no one is listening, so blend in."

Tink pulled a hat over her hair, hiding the brightly

89

coloured highlights. "No idea how this one will succeed in doing that." She pointed over to where Page was standing like a brick outhouse.

"I can be invisible when I need to be," he said, frowning. "Just ask my gran's carers whenever I bring up the subject of increasing her hours. It's like I'm no longer in the room."

"Well do what you can, both of you. The search will be going on until nightfall. Hopefully we find him before then."

Annie looked skyward; it was only the middle of the afternoon, but the light already seemed to be waning.

Tink and Page spread out into the crowds as the uniformed officers gave orders on the best way to conduct the search. Men, women and children lined the green and disappeared into the trees in a single file, covering a wide perimeter all eyes on the ground for clues.

"And us?" Annie asked, looking at Swift.

"We're going to find the two other names that keep popping up in this case. Windsor the museum guy, and the man who lives in the woods. Which one do you fancy first?"

"Let's follow the search and head into the woods," Annie said, intrigued by the man who would have had a direct view of anything happening on the lake where the boys had appeared. "I think someone living off the grid could be a good source of information. Not tainted by what he's reading online."

As it happened, Freddie Mold's wooden shack was better connected than Annie's own home. He had super-fast internet, a sky dish hidden around the back of the hut, and a million and one screens set up in a small nook beside a wood burner with a kettle boiling water on the top. What Freddie didn't have was patience for the police and the willingness to talk to them about anything whatsoever.

"Look officers," the man said as he poured hot water over what smelt to Annie like freshly picked mint leaves. "Like I said, I really can't help you."

He handed Annie a tin cup of mint tea and she took it gratefully, wrapping her fingers around it for the warmth. Even Swift sipped at the drink, his breath steaming around his face. Freddie Mold was hard to age, with his unkempt look and scraggy blonde beard he could be anything from twenty to sixty. What Annie could glean was that he was lean and wiry and that could have been down to malnutrition, or the sheer amount of exercise Freddie did simply breathing. He couldn't keep still.

"You have the perfect viewpoint of the lake from here, Mr Mold," Swift said. "And you're telling me you saw nothing when either Leon or Jacob emerged from the water? Or them going in in the first place? What have you seen recently that's given you cause to look twice?"

"Please call me Freddie, officers," Freddie replied,

his head swaying on his neck. "Mr Mold's my dad and he's a Grade A idiot."

Swift and Annie stayed silent, the ticking clock hanging from Freddie's wall the only sound.

"I know I have the perfect viewpoint of the lake," Freddie continued, picking at the skin around his thumb. "I chose this spot especially." Freddie stood from his chair and walked to the window, wiping away the haze with the sleeve of his jumper. He watched the water as it lapped gently at the stony shore, framed by the bare branches of the trees outside the hut. The line of the search party came into sight on the other side of the water and Freddie slid back down to his chair, a red flush rising on his face. "It's special to me, the lake, means everything to me."

Annie noticed the twitch in the man's leg, the way his eyes crossed the floor, avoiding both her and Swift.

"Why?" she prompted, gently.

"I've always been drawn to bodies of water," Freddie said. "And Lowanford Lake has healing powers. It's cleansing of the soul and of the mind. I have never seen anything by or in the water to give me cause for concern, officers. I'd tell you if I did because I want the lake to stay special. Sometimes when the teenagers are nearby I will watch them, just to make sure they're not doing anything they shouldn't, you know? And I know people talk about me as though I'm the odd one out in Lowan, but I'm just doing what's right for the lake and I don't bother nobody. The only people I saw on New Year's Eve were heading in the direction of the celebrations and they didn't go near the lake, they were on the road."

"Who was that?" Swift asked.

"Windsor, Hannah and her kids, as far as I can remember, that's it."

"And they'd normally pass by your hut…"

"It's my home, detective, not a hut, please treat it with respect," Freddie interrupted.

"Right," Swift carried out, eyebrow raised. "They'd normally pass by your *home,* would they, to get to the playing fields?"

Freddie nodded, placated. "Windsor always walks his dogs around the lake at that time of night and Hannah and her kids live this side of town, they often cut through the woods to get to the centre. Nice couple of kids them."

"And where were you all night?" Annie asked. "Did you go to the playing fields to watch the fire-works and see in the New Year?"

"They don't like me joining in, I'm not really welcome, haven't been really since I arrived a couple of years ago," Freddie said, his face dropping. "I keep myself to myself. I went to bed early and so my curtains were drawn most of the night."

Annie looked at the curtains in question, the flimsy material wouldn't keep out daylight, but she guessed they'd be hard to see out of if there was no light outside.

"Well thank you for your time, Freddie." Swift

stood and handed Freddie a card. "Please call us if you remember anything, no matter how insignificant it may seem."

Freddie turned the small card over in his hands, nodding. "Will do. And... um... can you tell me, was Jacob dead before he left the lake? Was his dead body in the water? How long for?"

"Call us," Swift said, shutting the door behind him and Annie and ignoring Freddie's question.

"That was an odd way to end things," Annie said when they were far enough away from the hut to talk.

"Odd talk in general," Swift said, leading them towards the row of people searching the floor of the woods.

"Do you think?" Annie said, stepping over a large dead branch. "I think he's just living his best life in the middle of nowhere, minding his own business."

"Except when there are teens around, then he minds *their* business."

Annie gave a noncommittal hum. "Point taken. But I think he truly lives near the water for the properties of the water and not the locals. What was it he said, that it was cleansing of the soul and mind?"

"Not of the body, though," Swift joked, and Annie had to laugh. Freddie hadn't been an obvious fan of personal hygiene.

"Not an arrestable crime, Joe," she said.

"No," he replied, stoically. "Let's go and talk to Windsor and see if we can get anything out of him instead. Nothing is making sense at the moment and we have so many loose strands, it's tying me up in knots."

"I'd say it's early days," Annie started. "But for Aaron, early days are the most important." She stopped and held out her hand to slow down the DI. "Look, Swift, I'd bet Sunday on that man being Windsor."

Swift barked out a laugh. "You'd bet your *cat* on it? O'Malley, I'm in my right mind to report you to the RSPCA."

Annie opened her mouth to remind Swift he'd left the poor creature alone when he flew to Majorca to help Annie last summer, but she wasn't quick enough.

"Mr Windsor?" Swift said loudly over the low chatter of the search party. "Can we have a word, please?"

The man Annie had her eye on turned to face them. Annie gave a single nod to Swift as a token that she wouldn't be giving Sunday away any time soon. Any man who wore a tweed suit to search through woodland was a historian in Annie's view. Thomas Windsor stepped away from the line of people and greeted the detectives with a smile.

"I was hoping you'd call on me," he said with words as neatly clipped as his hair.

"DI Swift and Annie O'Malley." Swift introduced them, moving away from the crowd and guiding Windsor with him. "Sorry to take you away from the search, we just have a few quick questions if we may?"

"Of course, of course, anything to help those poor boys," he replied, his face tinged slightly purple with the cold.

"What can you tell us about Aaron? About his relationship with Leon and Jacob?" Swift asked.

Windsor took a moment, not in a hurry to speak. Annie liked witnesses like Windsor, mostly people blurted out the first things that came into their heads when questioned by the police, afraid that they'd inadvertently do something wrong by not answering immediately. But Windsor didn't seem anxious about being arrested. He was either completely innocent or a great liar.

"Aaron Cooper is a boy who has been taken on a bit of a journey this year. Oh, excuse me officers, last year." Windsor gave a little laugh.

"What do you mean by that?" Annie asked.

"He's a good lad, only fourteen so he's a bit younger than the others. Used to help me out in the museum on a Saturday to earn a few pennies." As Windsor said this a pink flush spread over his face.

"It's okay Mr Windsor," Swift intervened. "We'll overlook the child labour for the moment."

Swift had a smile on his face, so Thomas Windsor continued on in good humour too. "He did a little dusting for a couple of pounds pocket money, I'm not running an enterprise like the outfit that is Kirkpatrick Constructions. Don't get me started on that man…

anyway, where was I? Oh yes, Aaron has made a few new friends this year and he's at that age now where image is king. I suppose we're all like that when we hit our teens."

"Were the new friends Leon and Jacob?" Annie asked.

Windsor shook his head. "No, those young lads have all been friends since they were very young, they grew up near each other, the four of them, Aaron, Leon, Jacob, and Noah. These are high school kids that Aaron's been hanging around with. Not a nice bunch. Not from 'round here. And I think Aaron might be dabbling with things he shouldn't, if you catch my drift?"

"Drugs?" Swift asked.

Windsor nodded.

"Do you know if any of the other boys were using drugs?"

"Maybe, I'm not sure."

"What makes you sure about Aaron?" Annie said.

"I found some evidence, shall we say. Down by the lake. I think it must have dropped out of Aaron's pocket as he was the only one there. It was a few months ago now. I tipped the pills down the toilet but there were so many of them it took a good few flushes."

Annie was scribbling furiously on her notepad, an idea germinating in her brain, remembering the phone they'd found and the image of naked women on the home screen.

"We understand you walked near the lake on New Year's Eve, is that correct?" Swift asked.

"That's right, I take the girls around the whole lake every evening no matter what the weather, they're spaniels so they need wearing out."

"I know that feeling," Swift agreed, laughing. "Though mine are labs, they're just as crazy."

Almost dropping her pen, Annie cocked her head in Swift's direction. She thought the dogs belonged to Sophia, Swift's ex-wife. Why was Swift walking them?

"And can you tell us if you saw or heard anything unusual?" Swift went on, oblivious to Annie's burning questions.

"Not that I can recall." Windsor pursed his lips and stroked his chin with a gloved hand. "I saw what I normally see on my walks; beautiful birds, the fisher-men, happy people of Lowan, it's a beautiful place to live. I don't understand why this is happening. It truly feels to me that ever since that scoundrel Kirkpatrick came to our town to look for places to build on, bad things have started happening."

Windsor was painting the picture of a children's book villain and he wasn't far off. Was Kirkpatrick the key to finding Aaron?

"He's on our radar," Swift said, thanking Windsor for his time.

"He needs to be on more than your radar, detectives. He needs to be locked up and the key thrown to the bottom of the lake."

If Kirkpatrick got his way, there would *be* no bottom of the lake anymore. Annie looked at the red spots growing on Windsor's cheeks and wondered if the small man in front of them knew of Kirkpatrick's real plans and how far he'd go to stop them.

ELEVEN

WEDNESDAY

"I<small>F</small> <small>ANYBODY KNOWS HOW TO STOP A DOG FROM</small> scratching at a bedroom door then please can they step forward now." Swift stood at the front of the incident room looking like he'd spent the night in Mold's hut. Unshaven, his hair standing on end, the bags under his eyes enough for a week in Spain.

"Keep it outside?" Page suggested, handing around the coffees.

Annie took her flat white and bit her tongue. She'd been in early again that morning, searching the system for a workaround for the restriction on her mum's file, and had made the executive decision that she was going to have to delve into the paper files to find anything accessible. There hadn't been time before the rest of the team had arrived and they'd all moved to the incident room.

"Any updates on the search for Aaron?" Annie asked, as they all settled down.

It was early, just gone eight and the sun was starting to make an appearance.

"The officers are back out there now," Tink replied. "And they're going door to door too, but they've got their work cut out. It poured last night, properly bucketing it down and that will have washed away any scent, so dogs are out of the question. Proper dogs, Swift, not those lazy beasts making themselves at home with you." She turned to their boss and blew him a kiss.

"Let's hope they find him." Swift picked up a marker and turned to the board. He wrote two additional names in bold lettering next to where Tink had already written Cameron Kirkpatrick. Thomas Windsor. Freddie Mold. "Here are the names that keep coming up. Annie and I have spoken to them all, Annie do you want to tell us about each of them?"

Annie nodded, gulping the rest of her coffee and taking her place at the front of the room. Never one for public speaking, Annie took a breath and got in the zone.

"Thomas Windsor. Local historian, owns the museum in Lowan. He's very proud of his town and is keen to stop any changes happening. He's embroiled in a dispute with Cameron Kirkpatrick who is what I'd call a nasty piece of work, though maybe not on record. We don't know a huge amount about Windsor or the history of Lowan so that's on our list of things to do today.

"Kirkpatrick is, as I said, not the nicest person in the world. He's loaded as far as the business is concerned. He'd hired all three of the boys who are involved in this case and he's on the warpath with Windsor because Kirkpatrick has his eye on Lowan land. He wants to fill in the lake and build houses."

"What?" Tink and Page exclaimed at the same time.

"Yep," Annie nodded. "He makes his money through property; my bet is that he has friends in high-up places as his construction sites are all on gold mines. So we need to look more into Kirkpatrick Constructions and I'd say we need to take a look at his accounts."

Swift nodded, sipping his coffee.

"I also think he has motive for hurting those boys," Annie went on, watching as Swift's brow creased. "If you think about it, Joe, the more Kirkpatrick sullies the lake and the water, the more likely it is he'll be able to get rid of it entirely. Dead teenagers are a sure-fire way to do that."

"That's extreme," Page whistled.

"Yeah," Annie went on. "But how many large building companies who throw up flimsy construc-tions and then sell or rent for a huge profit do you know with morals?"

"There's a big difference between fraud and

murder though," Swift added. "But you're right. We need to look into his business and him."

"Finally, we have Mold," Annie said, tapping the pen against Freddie Mold's name. "Reclusive, yes, odd, yes, but he eventually opened up to us and said he lives near the lake because he likes the properties the water offers. I think he's eccentric and has found somewhere he can live happily without being disturbed. But he does seem to keep a closer eye on the local teens than he needs to, and I think we need to look at his previous history too.

"All three men were around the lake at the time of Jacob's body appearing, and Mold and Windsor were there when Leon walked out of the water. They all have links with the boys. None of them have alibis for when the boys went missing, though we don't know exactly when that was."

"Any good news?" Page asked, a wry smile on his face.

Swift laughed. "I was hoping you guys might fill in some of the good news blanks. Thanks, Annie."

Annie took back her seat and got her notebook out to take notes when Page started to talk. Her underlined scribbles from the day before reminding her to add something. "Oh, Windsor mentioned the possibility that the boys, well Aaron at least, were using drugs. I'll be interested to hear if you guys have any more info on that lead."

Page looked to Swift for the nod to go ahead.

"Okay, so Tink and I have been looking into the

boys; their home lives, school lives, social media, that sort of thing." Page cleared his throat and wrote the boys' names on a new board before moving over to the suspects and adding a line under Kirkpatrick's name. "Though I want to say before I talk about them, I also looked into Cameron when his name first came up and he's got previous."

"Interesting," Swift said, steepling his fingers. "For what?"

"Common assault, aggravated assault, GBH," Page read out from his notebook. "If it's an anger issue, you name it."

"Wow, when were these charges?" Annie asked.

"They range, he's got a few dating back ten, fifteen years. Latest one was a couple years ago, a lesser Regulatory Investigative charge to do with declarations in Kirkpatrick Constructions but it was enough to make him move his business across county lines from Suffolk to Norfolk."

"Great, thanks Page. We definitely need more info on this company when you have time." Swift popped his lips, his thinking face on. "Okay, so the boys?"

Annie was still thinking about Cameron Kirkpatrick when Page started talking again, she flicked through to a blank page but not before underlining in hard pen the question *why is he so angry with Windsor?*

"Leon Scutts is doing well," Page said, smiling. "His body is starting to do more than the machines that were keeping him alive, which is great news. Still

104

not awake yet though. And the nurses are like Rottweilers anytime I go near him. His socials haven't given up much, nor have his emails. If I was to hazard a guess, I'd say these boys never booked themselves a holiday. They always had something else planned. He works for Kirkpatrick and is destined to do well in his exams. Tox results back and he was clear of alcohol and illegal drugs."

"Interesting," Annie muttered.

"His broken leg is healing and doctors think that was a very recent break, clean too, not a huge amount of bruising and no other injuries to make them think he was in an accident, car or bike, or a fall, etc."

"So how do they think he did it?" Annie asked.

"Something fell on his thigh, maybe. They don't like to say, they leave the deducting up to us." Page gave Annie a grimace. "But they're positive that he will pull through, though he may need a skin graft on some patches that have necrotised."

"That's really good news," Swift added, grabbing a pastry from the box. "In the main."

Page nodded, before dropping his eyes back to his notes. "Sadly, for Jacob, it was too late to save him. Jacob Mortimore, sixteen, was found at the edge of Lowanford Lake late in the day of the first of January. Almost twenty-four hours after Leon was found there alive. He was pronounced dead at the scene and transferred to the Norfolk and Norwich mortuary where Evans conducted his post-mortem. We haven't had the tox back yet for Jacob, I guess we could expedite

Leon's as he was still alive, and doctors needed them to make sure he stayed that way. You might need to get a rush on Jacob's, Swift, and now Aaron is missing we have probable cause to.

"Jacob was a friend of Leon, grew up together and hung out at work and at play. Different years in school, but Jacob was doing well with his studies and would have been taking his GCSEs this summer. Jacob died from septicaemia, blood poisoning, from open wounds in his arms and feet, indicating he'd been using intravenous drugs. He had no water on his lungs, but his body did show signs of having been in the water, so he was dead when he was dumped in the lake."

"How did he get out the water then?" Annie asked, curious, a little alarm bell ringing in her head.

"We're not sure yet," Page shrugged. "There are no other signs of injury, and he was in good health according to his parents and his GP records."

"Any recent behavioural changes?" Annie asked, thinking about what Windsor had told them about Jacob.

"Not ones that the family have volunteered, no."

"All good questions, O'Malley," Swift said, tapping his forefinger on the file in front of him. "But what's the burning question that we need to ask to move this investigation forward?"

Why you're walking your ex-wife's dogs? Annie felt her face flush and looked down at her hands, mind completely blank.

"Are the boys hurting themselves deliberately?" Tink answered, running a hand through her hair. "Jeez, I can't decide if I want them to be or not. The idea that these young men are doing something reckless and ending up dead is almost as bad as someone doing it to them. Shall I take over, Page?"

DC Page nodded, sitting down next to Swift with a puff of air. Swift patted him on the shoulder and Annie heard him whisper to the young DC that his sergeant's badge was a shoe-in.

"Aaron Cooper, younger than his local friends at just fourteen, missing possibly since last night, almost another twenty-four hours after Jacob was found. He's had a bit of a downward spiral recently, his sister said he's got in with the wrong crowd at their new high school, but his mum wasn't sure that's what the issue was. Though she couldn't spread any light on what she thought it could be. Like Annie said, maybe he'd been experimenting with drugs and wasn't sure which direction to go in? Aaron was there when Leon came out of the lake, so we can't rule out the fact he may have been in a bad headspace and just taken himself off somewhere to have a breather. But that could also be wishful thinking on our part. Worst case scenario, he's up to whatever those other boys were up to or has been taken by whoever took the others."

"Do we know why he didn't go on holiday with them?" Annie asked, before adding quickly. "Not holiday, I suppose, now we know they never booked it. But do we know why Aaron was never planning to go too, wherever it was they were going?"

"I asked his mum this," Tink replied. "And she said that Aaron was far too young to be going away without an adult. There was never any question around him going."

"From memory, I thought there were three of them going, but one couldn't afford it?" Annie asked, wracking her brains for where she'd heard that. "Was the third not Aaron, then?"

"Dropping a lot of balls this week, O'Malley," Swift said, grinning, and Annie felt her face heat again. "Did you overdo it with the eggnog over the holidays?"

Annie gave him a tight smile and started flicking through the pages of her notebook to see where she'd written it down.

"Here we go," she said, tapping the page with her forefinger. "I was right, there were three originally going to go, but one of them didn't as he doesn't have a job. His mum told us, do you remember Swift, when we were at the Mortimore's house after they realised Jacob was missing? The Brampton's son, Noah, was due to go too. His mum said he'd been under the weather too. Do you think there's a chance he could be in danger? Four friends from childhood; one dead, one in a coma, one missing?"

"I think it's something we need to consider, yes," Swift said, the smile wiped from his face. "And maybe he can tell us what it is that's tying them all together. I'll get an officer to stand at the door until we can get out there, but I want to talk to Kirkpatrick again first. He needs to open up a bit more about his business. Page, with me. Annie, Tink can you guys head to the museum and do a recce there? Talk to Windsor about Kirkpatrick and see what he knows about the plans for the lake."

Annie felt her stomach drop from her body. Was she really doing such a bad job that Swift didn't want her with him? She was going to have to pull it together and sort her head out because if Aaron turned up dead and she'd missed another chance to save a boy, Annie would never forgive herself.

TWELVE

They took Tink's car back to Lowan and parked up in the small car park designated for Lowan Museum visitors.

"I hope he opens on a Wednesday," Tink said, as they both stared at the dark windows and closed door to the museum.

It was a weird mix of old and new. A detached, squat building on the main road through the town, Lowan Museum had what seemed to be Tudor beams holding it together and a neon sign in the window. Neither of which looked like they were working.

Annie stepped up and tried the handle. Locked. She knocked loudly and stepped back, listening to any sounds beyond. It was quiet. The whole town seemed quiet; was everyone back out on the search for Aaron as the sun had started to rise?

"Maybe we should have rung ahead," Annie said. "Do you have Windsor's details on you?"

As Tink started to rummage around in the giant bag she carried everywhere, the door creaked open and Windsor's head poked through the gap.

"Oh, detectives, I wasn't expecting you, do forgive me." He shut the door in their faces.

The women looked at each other, eyebrows raised. But a few seconds later there was the noise of a lock sliding back and the door opened fully revealing Windsor in a pair of plaid pyjamas and leather slippers.

"Do come in, do come in." He ushered them through the door and closed it promptly behind them. "It's nippy out there."

They followed him through a tiny gift shop into the belly of the building where display cases held objects Annie couldn't quite see through the gloom.

"Please take a gander," Windsor said, flicking a light switch somewhere and illuminating both the whole room and the individual displays. "Michael has the kettle on, can he get either of you a drink while I go and get dressed? I feel rather foolish standing here in my jim jams."

He giggled and Annie liked the man even more than she already had done.

"I'd love a coffee please, white, no sugar," she replied, while Tink asked for a cup of strong builder's tea.

"I'll let Michael know, won't be long, detectives," Windsor said as he scuffled out the exhibition room in his slippers.

"Oh my goodness, he's so sweet," Tink said, heading to a large wall display depicting a timeline of the town.

"Kirkpatrick would disagree with you," Annie said, going to join her.

"Kirkpatrick sounds like a man I'd like to disagree with quite a lot," Tink whispered, making sure the museum was empty first.

The timeline was printed on a large white board, colourful arrows and pictures depicting the history of the small mining community. Grubby faced workers smiled from underneath their hard hats; black and white photos of cave-like structures; a pencil sketch of the galvanised mine shafts and layers of sands and flints; and more modern pictures of the local houses. Annie leant in, peering at the most recent photo of the town and the lake, noticing the divots along the playing field, a throwback to the holes dug in the ground to reach the flint.

"Can't imagine that's easy to play sports on," she said, nodding to the picture.

"Weird how you can't see those divots when you're walking on it," Tink agreed. "And look at the lake, they've captured its glow really well in this photo. Do you think it's photoshopped?"

"Tommy would never allow it, not in here." The voice made both the women jump and turn to see who'd spoken. "Sorry, sorry. I wasn't setting out to scare you. I'm Michael, with your drinks." He handed Annie and Tink their cups and stood back to admire the timeline. "No, that photo is what the lake looks like whenever it's dark. Just the photoshopping by Mother Nature herself."

"Do you think the lake has powers?" Annie asked, sipping her coffee, surprised by how delicious it was.

"I think it's got something," Michael said, turning to Annie. "Whether that's healing powers or whether it's just the suggestion of healing powers, if it works, then that's good enough for me. I can't imagine why the locals are not doing more to stop that awful man, Kirkpatrick and his plans. Now, if you'll excuse me, I'm sure Tommy will be back soon. He normally loves a long shower in the mornings but I'm sure he'll be less vigorous with his cleansing today as he knows you're down here waiting for him."

Michael gave them both a wink and disappeared back through a doorway hidden in the darkness.

"Kirkpatrick is definitely not a welcome man in Lowan Museum," Tink said, moving around to a display case with a range of pieces of flint highlighted by singular bulbs and name plates.

"He's not a welcome man in Lowan." This time it was Windsor who made them jump.

Annie's coffee sloshed over the brim of her mug and warmed her fingers. She transferred her cup to the other hand and wiped the drips on her trousers to stop them falling on the immaculate carpet or she might find herself on a par with Kirkpatrick in Windsor's eyes.

"Do you know what he's planning?" Windsor

asked them, not waiting for an answer. "He wants to fill the lake in, to turn it into houses. He's ruined countless other small towns like ours with his greed and shoddy workmanship. Selling them off for a profit and then leaving as they all start to crumble. Why, only the other side of Fakenham there's a lawsuit in the making. Houses tilting like the Tower of Pisa because Kirkpatrick can't be bothered with foundations." Windsor took a breath and pulled on a smile. "Sorry, you're not here to talk to me about Kirkpatrick, are you? You're here to see the museum."

Bit of both, Annie thought, before saying. "How many visitors do you get to your museum, Mr Windsor?"

"Oh, you'd be surprised," Windsor said, leading them to a display case filled with flints of all shapes and sizes. "We have quite an online following here in Lowan. People often email the museum and ask us to send them vials of the lake water. To which I, of course, say no." Windsor laughed softly. "Can you imagine the mess? Not to mention, we like them to come here to see the lake for themselves and not just use it for their own means. The museum isn't here to make a profit, we're here to raise awareness of the town's fabulous history and its even more fabulous present."

"What's your favourite part of Lowan's history, Mr Windsor?" Tink asked, looking engrossed by a tiny piece of flint in the shape of a heart.

"We think that was a sign," Windsor said, tapping the glass. "The heart. I found it while I was walking, years and years ago. It was by the edge of the lake, at the top, the part that's more difficult to get to, I'm not sure if you've been up there yet?" The women shook their heads and Windsor continued. "I liked the way it held meaning for the lake and was made from the blood and bones of what Lowan is renowned for. Flint and heart. Hey, that would be a good name for a pub if I ever want to change my career. But to answer your question, my dear, my favourite piece of Lowan history is the way the town shifts itself with the times. We went from being an industrious mining town where stone was mined for houses all over the county and the country eventually. When the mines were dry and the lake was created on a large part of the dugout countryside, it proved itself once again. The land turned the lake into something special that encourages people to visit and it builds a community for the people of Lowan. Whenever we've needed it, the land has provided."

Annie nodded, she looked at the heart shaped flint, the curved edges where the water had bashed away the razor sharpness. "And what do you think will happen if Kirkpatrick's plans to fill in the lake are approved? Will Lowan be able to rebuild itself, given that it's done it once already?"

Windsor's face pinched in distaste. "He won't get approval. Not if I've got anything to do with it. And especially now with what's happened with these boys."

Tink looked up from the display at Windsor. "What do you mean?"

A flush spread across Windsor's cheeks as he ran a hand over his hair, patting it down neatly. "I just mean that, well, of course, these parents won't want the lake filled in because it's a place for them to go and reflect on their boys' lives. A memorial if you like?"

"It's only Jacob that's dead, Mr Windsor," Annie said, slowly, easing herself back upright and looking at the curator with different eyes. "Do you think that Leon's mum would want to go and remember how her son was deposited out of the lake half dead and bloated by the water? I know I wouldn't. And what about Aaron? Is there something you need to tell us, Mr Windsor?"

"Oh my goodness, what a fluster," Windsor replied, flapping at his red face with a useless hand. "That's not what I meant. I was just hoping that something good for the town would come out of this tragedy, do you see? That this would stop Kirkpatrick from having his own way? But I can see how what I said might look and I apologise."

Annie felt sorry for the man, but she didn't allow this to get in the way of the alarm bells ringing in her head. She'd been so quick to point fingers at Kirkpatrick and the ways he'd be able to fill in the lake, that Windsor's slightly obsessive love of Lowan hadn't crossed her mind as a cause for concern.

"We'll be in touch, Mr Windsor," she said, handing her empty mug to the man. "Please do call us if there's anything else you can think of from New Year's Eve."

Windsor nodded, his eyes filling with tears. "I will, of course I will. There's really nothing out of the ordinary that I can think of. Just the normal goings on around the lake. The teenagers hanging out. People packing away their fishing stuff for the evenings. Mr Mold taking a walk to the water. I am sorry, truly I am, about what is happening to these boys."

Annie and Tink took their leave and headed out into the bright, freezing sunshine. The day was well and truly awake, and Annie felt a weight lift from her shoulders as they emerged into the light.

"I don't know about you," she said to Tink. "But that museum needs an update and some windows."

Tink laughed and beeped her car unlocked. "You can't have windows in museums, Annie, sunlight ruins the items on display. Even if it is a bunch of stones. And talking of stones. I'd like to take another look at the lake, if we can? I know the search teams are looking all around, and forensics are doing what they can given the circumstances, but I'd really like to walk the whole way around and see if there's anything we've missed."

"Sounds like a plan," Annie agreed, because if

there were as many people out by the lake as Windsor had said, then surely at least one of them must have seen something. Either that, or they're hiding something.

THIRTEEN

Though Annie had already walked along the south edge of Lowanford Lake, it stretched much further than she'd initially realised, disappearing into the woods the further around they looked. The two detectives flashed their badges at the officer guarding the scene and he held up the tape for them to pass through. Groups of locals were still out looking for Aaron on the outskirts of the crime scene tape, working in lines as they'd been instructed the day before. Inside the tape was a different matter.

A chill washed over Annie as she watched the heads of a small team of frogmen bobbing about on the surface of the water, listening to commands from their superior watching them from a boat. They'd gotten to the stage of the search where they needed to expect the worst and were searching the depths of the water near to where the two other boys had been found.

A chirruping from Annie's phone startled her and she drew it out of her pocket to see the familiar name of Swift flash up on the screen.

"Hiya," she answered, trying not to let the hope show in her voice.

"Hey, O'Malley, it's Swift," came the reply. "We didn't get anything useful out of Kirkpatrick, he's asking for his lawyer now, even for informal chats so we can't bring him in unless we have something concrete. Page and I are heading back to Lowan, can you meet me at the Brampton's place in a couple of hours? I'll text you the address and let you know when I'm there."

"Sure," Annie said. "See you there."

Annie hung up and pocketed her phone, catching up to Tink as close to the edge of the water as she could go with the active crime scene.

"Swift?" Tink asked.

Annie nodded and the two women started their search around the perimeter of the lake, heading first in the direction of Freddie Mold's shack.

"I was surprised when you guys didn't see in the new year together," Tink said, throwing Annie off guard.

"Why?" She sounded more defensive than she'd meant to. But Annie had never talked to Tink about her feelings for Swift because Tink had known him a lot longer and had worked with him for years. Annie didn't want to come in and unsettle the apple cart, not

120

when it was rooted and full of delicious fruit ready to be spoiled.

"Oh, no reason, just… you know… you guys get on really well." Tink had a twinkle in her eye but she changed the subject before Annie could answer. "Anyway, let me guess, Swift didn't get anywhere with Kirkpatrick?"

Annie laughed with relief. "He's one of those guys who talks the talk but can't handle it when things get tough."

"Do you think he's hiding something?"

Annie took a moment to think about the savvy businessman who was as smarmy as he was cocky. There had been something about the way he'd skirted questions and given pithy answers that had set Annie's teeth on edge. "Yeah, I do."

Tink looked over at her, eyebrows raised. "He's a nasty piece of work. Nasty enough to kill to get what he wants?"

"Oh god, yeah. I've no doubt he would go to any lengths to make more and more money. People like him have no scruples. He's like a poor man's wannabe gangster, or at least he thinks he is."

"I can sense a but…" Tink stopped as the trees encroached on the path, their branches too thick to walk easily side by side.

"But those boys?" Annie shrugged. "I just can't see what killing or hurting them would achieve. Not money. I can't imagine he's sending a message to other developers by hurting them. They were working for Kirkpatrick, probably for a pittance, why get rid of them?"

Tink's eyes widened. "Maybe we're looking at this from the wrong angle, maybe you've just hit the nail on the head. Why would Kirkpatrick want to get rid of three boys who worked for him if it wasn't to gain something?"

Tink pushed back the branches of a gnarly looking tree and let Annie go first.

"To hide something?" Annie's mind was whirring. "Maybe this has less to do with the development of the site and more to do with something else that Kirkpatrick is planning that the boys found out?"

"Or maybe it's both?" Tink said. "I know we're jumping the gun a bit here with theorising what ifs, but really, what exactly do we have on this case? What are our leads?"

Annie stepped carefully over the thick foliage underfoot, picking the route that was the easiest to walk but was taking them slightly away from the water. It was still close enough to see, though, grey and rather forlorn looking during the day. A vast world away from the magical scenes it depicted when the sun dropped below the horizon.

"Cameron Kirkpatrick and his development," Annie started. "Freddie Mold and his fascination with teenagers. Thomas Windsor and his inherent need to protect his town. Then there are the boys themselves. Where had they been? Why did they lie? And what were they planning?"

122

"And where has Aaron gone?" Tink added quietly.

"Arguably the most important question right now." Annie turned and headed in the direction of the water again, the path clearer up ahead. "We need to talk to Aaron's sister and find out what she knows. And I'm meeting Swift at the Brampton's house when he gets here from Kirkpatrick's place, we can talk to their son too. Kids always protect each other, but when it comes down to it, surely they want to find their friend?"

Tink hummed in agreement as they broke out of the tree line and found themselves back in the open by the edge of the water. The lake stretched out in both directions, to their left in the distance were the frogmen, ready to dive. To their right, the tip of the north side of the lake, a couple of walkers, their coats flashing colour against the brown backdrop of the trees, and a lone fisherman patiently watching for a catch.

"Let's go and say hi," Annie said, her feet crunching over the shingle. "Someone out here would have a great view of the whole of the water. Maybe they know something or saw something."

"Pretty sure uniform have taken statements from everyone who was around the lake at any point in the recent past."

"Good, then we'll wheedle extra information out of them, you're good at that." Annie gave Tink a gentle nudge with her shoulder.

"Not as good as I'd like to be," Tink replied, a wry smile on her face.

The fisherman looked up from what seemed to be a trance in the direction of the still waters, as the detectives approached. He wiped a hand down his damp jacket and offered it up to Annie who was glad of her gloves as she shook it.

"Good morning," she said, introducing herself and Tink. "Is it okay if we ask you a few questions?"

"Of course," he replied, smiling through blue lips. "You'll have to excuse me if I get a hook, though, I tend to forget where I am with the excitement."

"Do you catch a lot?" Annie asked, noticing the smile on the fisherman's face.

"No, rarely. We don't really come out here for the fish." The man laughed, a beefy laugh that matched his ruddy face. "Don't tell our wives that though."

He tapped his finger on his nose.

"Of course," Annie said, conspiratorially, secretly glad he'd been so open. She loved having bartering material. "You said we?" She gestured around to the empty shoreline.

"Me and my bucket of bait," the man said which made Tink snort. "No, there are sometimes two or three of us. But with the goings on, today it's just me. And I don't blame them. Ed is at home with his wife and son, he's a similar age to the boys who've... well, you know better than anyone. And Grant's wife said he'd be showing the family up if he carried on fishing here like nothing had happened."

"And you?" Annie prompted. "We didn't catch your name."

"Paul," he said. "My wife enjoys having me out the house as much as I enjoy being here." He laughed again and Annie wondered if Paul would be at home in the warmth if he got on better with his wife.

"Are you out here most days?" Annie had figured that Paul would be retired, given his white hair and wrinkles but he shook his head.

"Oh no, we all work, tend to come here on a weekend."

"It's Wednesday." Tink looked confused.

"A guy is allowed to take holiday." He winked at Tink.

"Were you here in the run up to New Year?" Annie asked. "New Year's Eve?"

"Yep, and before you ask, no we didn't see anything. Ed had his tent, sensible chap. Grant was three sheets to the wind on home-brew. And I was doing the actual fishing."

"And you didn't see or hear anything unusual?" Tink asked.

"Nothing unusual, no. There was the usual crowd, Windsor pretending to walk his dog whilst actually following Kirkpatrick and his builder around the lake. Mold was out here too, but that's nothing special. He was filling his containers with lake water. God knows what he does with it all, he's always up there with his old water bottles and those drums that hold industrial amounts of cooking oil. Wheelbarrow and everything.

It's annoying because he disturbs the water when he's doing it, scares away the fish, doesn't he?"

Annie chuckled, tucking away the information for later. "And what's scaring them away right now?"

"You two," Paul joked. "To be honest, I'm not sure there's even fish in this lake. It's man-made so we'd have had to add the fish too."

Annie rolled her eyes.

"Have you been told it's okay to continue to fish here, what with the searches going on? Isn't it dangerous for the divers?" Tink said, nodding to the south shore.

"They said for the time being it's okay," he replied.

"And if you catch something… that perhaps might be connected to the case?" Annie added.

Paul shook his head. "Unlikely, my dear. None of us actually use hooks."

They thanked the fisherman for his time and headed on further on around the lakeshore to the northern tip of the water.

"It's like golfing," Tink said as the terrain got rockier and harder to navigate. "I just don't under-stand it."

"It's a way of men spending time with each other without having to feel awkward about it," Annie replied. "Probably, anyway. The younger generations are much better at talking about how they're feeling and reaching out to their friends. But men like Paul and I'm guessing

Ed and Grant, they're of a generation who were told to grit their teeth and get on with life no matter what. Activities that get them out the house and hanging out with each other is a good thing. I can't imagine they actually enjoy sitting in the damp and cold."

"You can tell you used to be a therapist," Tink laughed.

"What do you mean, used to?" Annie said, smiling. "I still am."

But now that Tink had said it, Annie wondered if she could still work as effectively with the old clients she used to as a psychotherapist; mostly young men on parole. Or even, as she had a mild panic about it, if she'd renewed her registration with the clinical body that governed her profession. She added it to the growing list of things to do that she kept stored in her head which reminded her about something Paul had said.

"Tink," she called over her shoulder. "Did you notice what the fisherman said about Windsor?"

"That he followed Kirkpatrick around pretending to walk his dogs?" Tink called back.

Annie nodded and concentrated on the path as it flattened out again and opened up to the northern tip of the lake.

Underfoot was a mix of shingle and larger pieces of flint. "Watch your step," Annie called again. "These rocks are sharp."

"Annie?" There was something in the tone of

Tink's voice that made Annie stop in her tracks, her blood running as cold as the water beside them.

She turned to look at the DS who was crouching down on the shingle, eyes trained on something glistening beneath the stones.

"What is it?" Annie stepped closer.

"We need uniforms here," Tink said, looking up at Annie. "We need to close off the whole perimeter of this lake. Look at this."

Annie looked down as Tink took out her phone and started taking photographs to document what she'd found. Peeking out through the shingle was a mobile phone. The screen was cracked and dead, but that didn't stop the sunlight reflecting from the water, highlighting the drops of blood dried onto the glass.

FOURTEEN

By the time Annie and Tink left the lake, uniformed officers were clearing away any people who were still there and the area cordoned off by the crime scene tape had been widened. The mobile phone was bagged and tagged and was being whisked back to the lab for analysis on the blood and finger-prints before it would be couriered to the tech team to try and extract some information. It could be a lost phone from anyone from any time, but both Annie and Tink had a bad feeling about it and would do even if it wasn't tainted with blood.

"Sorry, sorry," Annie said, breathlessly, jogging towards where Swift and Page were waiting by Swift's car. The playing fields were still a hub of activity but the general chatter from the public had died down as the whispers of what had been found were doing the rounds.

The sun shone brightly overhead, crisping the

damp away and shining a spotlight on Swift as though he were centre stage.

"Stop running," Tink shouted. "It's not like we're late back because we were having a jolly."

Annie slowed to let Tink catch up and they walked the last few yards together.

"Good find, Tink," Swift said, clapping her on the shoulder. "Makes me wonder why it hadn't been found already though."

"I think it had been covered in shingle," Tink replied. "Not easy to see when the weather hasn't been so bright. The sun has done us a favour today."

"I've tried to expedite the results from the lab but given we're still waiting for Jacob's tox results I don't know how long it'll take to analyse the phone."

Swift encouraged his team to huddle together and told them that they were trying to build a case against Kirkpatrick to bring him in so they could question him properly.

"Has that come from Robins?" Annie asked, brow creased.

Swift nodded. "She said we need some results, apparently Kirkpatrick has friends in high places and they're breathing down her neck."

Annie smiled. "What, so she's going after one of their own? I like her style."

"Tink and Page, can you guys head back to the hospital and see what's happening with Leon? I've also tried to set up a meeting with Maisie, Aaron's sister, but the parents are vetoing it for now because

130

she's so traumatised apparently, maybe do a bit of subtle digging on the girl, see what you can get from her friends, teachers, pets," Swift said. "Annie we're going to talk to the Brampton boy, see what he can tell us about his friends. Someone, somewhere must know what the hell these boys have been up to."

He looked riled; cheeks pink, eyes wide, as he turned to unlock his car. Annie followed, waving goodbye to Tink and Page as they headed back to the city.

Inside Swift's car was warm and comfortable and as Annie sat down her stomach growled and her bones ached. She'd been out since the crack of dawn and had only had two cups of coffee and a pastry to keep her going. Given that the car clock was telling her it was nearly lunch time, it was no wonder her stomach was complaining.

"There's a sandwich in the back," Swift said, putting the car in reverse and pulling out of the playing field.

Annie grabbed the M&S bag and pulled out not just any sandwich but a favourite of hers in the shape of a bacon, brie, and cranberry baguette and pretty much inhaled it as Swift drove the short distance to the Brampton's house.

Given the size of the houses in Lowan, the Brampton's were either old money, or doing very well for themselves. Their home looked nothing like the run of terraces or the older cottage style homes in the town centre, it was an elegant seventies home with a gated driveway made in brick and tile with no flint to be seen.

Swift pulled up to the gate and wound down his window, pressing the button to call the house.

"Yes?" A voice crackled over the speaker. Annie couldn't tell if it was male or female.

Swift gave their names and the gate started to slide open.

"You should get one of these," Annie said. "You could vet who you let in before they ring your doorbell."

She was saying it in jest because Swift's home was a mansion on the outskirts of Norwich that he still hadn't divulged how he afforded to buy. But he looked like he was contemplating the idea as he pulled up through the gate posts and circled the car in front of the house.

"That's not a bad idea, O'Malley," he said as they got out. "I could have done with that this Christmas."

"Carol singers?" she asked, ringing the doorbell.

"Not quite." Before he could tell her who was turning up uninvited to his home, the door to the Brampton's edged open and a familiar face peered out.

"Mrs Brampton, do you remember us, we met at the Mortimore's home," Annie said, gently as the woman looked on the edge of a nervous breakdown. "I'm so sorry for the loss of your friends' boy. May we come in?"

She pulled the door wider, nodding. "Please do. Excuse the mess."

There was no mess. The home was as immaculate on the inside as it had looked on the outside. Neat cream carpets lined the floors of every room, silver picture frames on dust free sideboards held photos of the family, soft lighting filled the spaces making it feel homely and friendly and as Annie followed the woman through to the living room, she felt her shoulders drop from around her chin.

"Have a seat, can I get you anything to drink?" Mrs Brampton asked as Annie and Swift sat next to each other on a large navy sofa under a long window.

Even if neither of them wanted a refreshment, they mostly said yes because they knew it would give them time to nosy around without eyes watching their every move. They put in their requests and waited for the coast to clear.

"What a lovely home," Annie said, getting off the sofa and heading to look at a bookshelf in the corner of the room with a collection of photos on the top.

There was a small silver tray with medicine bottles stacked neatly, handwritten labels turned outwards, so their edges lined up perfectly. She picked up a hinged frame with a wedding photo of Mr and Mrs Brampton on one side and the couple holding a newborn baby on the other. Putting it back down, Annie looked at the others. Dust free pictures of the Brampton family throughout their son's growth, from baby to toddler to child to teen. In a recent picture, taken at the edge of the lake, the youngest of the Brampton's had his arms flung over the shoulders of two boys Annie recognised, Jacob and Aaron.

"Look at this, Swift," Annie said, lifting the photo carefully from the ones surrounding it and holding it out to the DI. "They look like good friends."

"We are good friends. At least, we were." Turning to see who'd spoken, Annie knocked against the bookshelf, wobbling all the frames. "Don't let mum see you getting fingerprints all over her silverware, she'll kick you out before you've had your coffee."

The boy looked to be in his early teens before the ravages of hormones and spots had landed. He was skinny, pale, and tall, and undoubtedly his mother's son. Their eyes were the same shade of liquid green.

"DI Swift, Annie O'Malley," Annie said, holding her hand out to who she figured was the youngest Brampton himself, Noah. "Thanks for the heads up." She wiped the frame on her jumper and placed it back down on the bookshelf. "I'm so sorry for the loss of your friend. You and Jacob look close."

Noah nodded, sadly, and slumped with the grace of a teenager onto the free sofa. Annie sat back down next to Swift, and they both waited for the young man to open up to them. It didn't take long, which Annie was glad of, but she glanced sideways at Swift to remind him that Noah was underage.

"Do you want to wait for your mum to come back, Noah?" Annie asked when Swift stayed silent.

Noah shook his head. "Not unless I'm under

arrest?" he said, laughing and holding out his wrists for them to cuff. His laugh rattled, turning into a cough that wracked his whole body.

"Your mum said you'd been under the weather," Annie said as Noah regained control of his lungs. "Is that why you didn't go with your friends last week?"

"Kinda," he tilted his head from side to side, biting his bottom lip. "But, my mates never asked me neither."

"Is that unusual?" Swift asked.

"Yeah," Noah went on. "We do everything together. Me, Leon, Aaron, and Jacob."

At the mention of the dead boy, Noah's voice cracked. He cleared his throat and took a deep breath, gaining composure.

"They didn't really tell me much about what they were doing, just that they were heading off for a few days." Noah chewed on the inside of his cheek. "I figured it was something to do with work and that's why I wasn't allowed to go."

"Their work at Kirkpatrick Constructions?" Annie asked and Noah nodded.

"Ever since they started working there, they got really weird, like."

"In what way?"

"Secretive, they'd have these inside jokes that I couldn't get. Not that I minded, I just wish I could have worked with them too, that's all. It seemed like fun and they had loads of cash to spend."

"Why didn't you want to get a job with them?"

Swift said as Mrs Brampton came back into the room with a tray of steaming hot mugs.

"Oh Noah, love, you're up?" she said, her face brightening with the sight of her son. "Let me just get these lovely detectives their drinks and I'll fetch you some lunch."

Noah's cheeks reddened and he shrugged as though he didn't care about his lunch. "Not hungry, thanks."

"Well let me at least get you a drink?" Mrs Brampton flustered around with the tray, putting it heavily down on the large coffee table with a clatter.

"Mum, give over, I can get my own drink."

Annie took her mug silently and pretended to look at something interesting out of the smaller window on the other side of the room while the family dramas came to a close. As the room stilled and calmed, Annie drew her eyes back to the mother and son sitting together opposite. She felt for Mrs Brampton wanting to look after her only child given the circumstances, but she also remembered how painfully embarrassing parents were as a teenager.

"Noah was just telling us about the boys' work, remind us again why you weren't working there too?" Annie prompted, sipping her coffee.

Noah stuck out his chin and glared at his mum. "She won't let me."

It was Mrs Brampton's turn to flush.

"I don't like the man," she said, as steely as her son. "There's something about the way he works that irks me. And those boys had far too much money in their pockets for labourers, you mark my words." Mrs Brampton turned to her son. "Besides, you're under the weather at the moment, listen to that chest of yours. Better off in here in the warmth."

Noah rolled his eyes and sat back with crossed arms.

Annie gave Mrs Brampton a knowing smile but tried to direct her back to what she'd said about the money. "Can you tell me what you mean about how much Kirkpatrick was paying the boys, Mrs Brampton?"

"Well, they just seemed to have rather a lot of it, that's all." She looked down into her cup. "God rest Jacob's soul. Poor thing. The last time I saw him, his wallet was bursting at the seams with notes. Not mangy old used ones either. They were crisp and clean and they made alarm bells go off in my head."

Mine too, thought Annie.

"I'd rather the boys stayed local, hung out together around each other's houses, or by the lake," she finished, taking her cup from the tray and sipping slowly.

Noah snorted loudly, startling them all. Annie saw Swift's drink slosh close to the rim of the cup, not quite tipping over the edge. Mrs Brampton, on the other hand, was teetering on the edge of whatever it was she was walking. Her eyes filled with tears, and she looked to the ceiling to stop them from falling.

"You'd rather we stayed local?" Noah sneered,

ignoring the pain his mum was in. "What, so that perv Mold can carry on filming us through the trees. Like he thinks we don't know. God knows what he's doing while he's filming. Or what he does with the footage. But I bet I can take a good guess."

He made a rude gesture and Mrs Brampton's face flushed even redder.

Annie turned to Swift, whose face gave him away. They were both thinking the same thing. It was reason enough to pull the man in for questioning. Because why was he filming teenagers? And what else had he caught on tape?

FIFTEEN

It was late by the time Annie and Swift arrived back at the station. With Tink and Page still up at the hospital, and a rather angry Freddie Mold waiting for them in the interview room, Annie didn't take her time unwrapping herself from her cold coat and gloves and warming up in the office before she faced him.

"Did we ever get any info on Mold's past, do you know?" she asked Swift as they made their way to the interview rooms.

"Nothing," Swift replied. "His history is clean."

"As far as we're aware?" Annie said and Swift nodded glumly.

"We're getting a warrant to search his hut and take in his IT gadgets, there was enough of them, do you remember?"

"Yep," Annie said, thinking about the screens Mold had in the living area of his hut, and the super-speed modem. "It's all adding up to a very grim picture, isn't it?"

Swift grunted and stopped at the interview room door, turning to look at Annie.

"This isn't going to be under caution, not yet. So we need to make him talk until we have something we can pin him with. At the very least we need him to offer to hand over any footage he has."

Annie nodded, looking closely at Swift's face, the way his blue eyes always darkened whenever he was angry. They steeled themselves then threw open the door to the interview room and descended upon Freddie Mold like detectives on a mission.

"Mr Mold," Swift started before they'd even sat down. "We need you to start being honest with us. And we need you to do that now. There is a boy's life at stake and you're withholding important... no, not even just important, *vital*, information from us that could potentially save his life. What do you know about what happened to these boys?"

Mold didn't look like a man in a hurry to help. He leant back in his chair, his head tilted to the side, his mouth drawn into a small smile.

"You're stuck, aren't you?" he said, his voice reedy and thin. "That's why you're grasping at straws? Let me tell you this, detectives, those boys, the missing boy, they have nothing to do with me. Nothing at all. They're just out to cause trouble."

"Then why are you so interested in them?" Annie

asked, leaning forward, her elbows propped on the desk.

"I'm not interested in them." Mold's eyes narrowed.

"We have reason to believe otherwise." Swift sat forward too, looming over Mold.

"What reason?" He was looking warier now, eyes shifting between Annie and Swift.

"Reports that you've been filming them," Annie said, watching carefully for any tell-tale signs that this was a false allegation. None came. Mold wasn't surprised.

"It's up to me what I film, the lake and the woods don't belong to anyone, do they?"

"It's against the law to film people without their knowledge." In actual fact, Annie had no idea if that was true, but it sounded like it should be.

"Why those boys, Mold?" Swift's voice was low and probing. "What is it about them that attracts you?"

Now that got a reaction from the man. Mold's face whitened and he pushed himself upright in the chair.

"Wait a minute," he said, clearing his throat. "What do you mean *attracts?*"

"You tell us," Swift went on.

"No, no, don't you dare taint me with that brush. What I'm doing has nothing to do with… oh god, you can't think I'm one of those." Mold twisted his hands over themselves, the red raw skin at the tips of his fingers blooming white with the pressure. "I'm not attracted to boys or any child for that matter. Just because I live an off-the-grid life that's different from what society dictates is normal, that doesn't mean you can point a finger at me and call me a paedophile."

Annie cocked her head in annoyance. "Mr Mold, we're not trying to figure out if you're attracted to young boys because you live in a hut in the middle of nowhere, we're asking because you've been caught filming them. And a little FYI for you, being off-the-grid normally requires no internet or phone or electricity, hence the name. You're as off the grid as we are here in the station. Mr Mold you have more TV screens than I do at home."

He relaxed a little at that, but still looked as wary as a mouse at a cat's tea party. His fight or flight response kicking in.

"I very rarely video the boys," he said, quietly, slumping back in his chair. "Only when they're irritating me do I threaten them with it. But recently… well I'm quite glad I did."

A cog clicked into place in Annie's head, something that Windsor had said back in the museum about his file of evidence and having someone on the inside.

"How long have you lived in the hut?" she asked, piqued.

"It's not a hu…," Mold saw the look on Annie's face and sighed. "Oh, okay, it's a bloody hut. I don't always live there, I've got a home in the next village over."

"And who does it really belong to?" she asked.

"All the equipment and the cameras? You're no more a nomad than I am."

She caught Swift looking across at her out of the corner of her eye and wondered if she should have stepped out with him when she realised what was going on. But he's always trusted her instincts before, and this time should be no different.

"The hut is mine," Mold replied, but he wasn't arguing anymore. "I bought it years ago thinking it would be a prime piece of real estate to build a proper house on. Then I came up against Thomas Windsor and that was that."

"He's a man with Lowan at his heart, isn't he?" Annie said, not really a question.

Mold nodded. "He said over my dead body would I be allowed to build near his precious lake. So I kept it just to piss him off, stayed in it when I could. Then a couple of years ago he came to me for help."

"To spy on Kirkpatrick?" Anne asked.

Mold nodded again. "That man is corrupt as hell and without evidence to prove it, Kirkpatrick would raze Lowan and all who live there to the ground. He has friends on the council planning, which is why all his projects get the go-ahead."

"So you and Windsor joined forces?" Swift had decided to enter into the conversation and Annie could practically hear the cogs whirring in his head. "You've been filming Kirkpatrick to try and catch him out and finally have something to stop his plans for Lowan?"

143

"Yes." Mold looked down at his hands.

"And you have cameras hidden in the trees?"

"Not cameras, no, they're all in my hut. But we do have microphones."

"We're going to need any recordings that you have from the last few weeks and anything else that you have of interest. Do you listen to the recordings before you send them to Windsor?"

Mold's face was returning to a normal shade, he seemed to be a man whose secrets had weighed him down to a shell, and sharing these secrets had given him a new lease of life.

"Sometimes I do," he said. "But a lot of it is boring building talk and Kirkpatrick isn't a modest man, shall we say that. Listening to him harp on about how much money he's going to make from the land is sickening and there's only so much of it I can stomach."

"Did you find anything incriminating about how he's going about getting authorisation to build on the land and fill in the lake?" Annie asked. "Maybe the boys overheard something and that's put them in danger?"

"Nothing to date, as far as I know," Mold said, shaking his head. "And I wouldn't put it past some of the boys who hang out by the lake to do something with info like that. But not Leon, or the others, they're good boys. They're always doing what they can to help their families, I can't see them causing trouble."

"It's amazing what money can make people do

though," Annie said, her little grey cells unravelling another strand of this unusual case. There was something that was troubling her and she couldn't put her finger on it, not yet.

Mold gave an ironic laugh and tried to disguise it as a cough.

"What is it?" Annie asked.

"I lived in a hut for money," Mold shrugged. "Though I have to say, since washing in the lake water my skin has never been better. I used to get eczema and that's all but cleared up. My hair has also grown at a rate of knots. There's something in the water that I'm going to miss when I go back home."

Mold's words jolted the strand of thought in Annie's brain into a graspable entity and she knew all at once what it was that had been troubling her.

"Is that why you've been collecting the water in containers?" Swift asked as Annie figured out how to word her question.

"Some for me, some for Windsor. He likes to make his morning drinks with it."

Annie felt her stomach turn remembering the coffee she'd drunk earlier, then she broached the subject.

"Is that why you asked us, in your hut the other day, if Jacob had been dead when he was in the water?" she asked, feeling queasy.

Mold's face gave him away. He may have been nodding but Annie knew there was more to his question than he was saying.

"Mr Mold, can you tell me why, exactly, you asked if Jacob was already dead when he entered the water?" she asked.

Mold's eyes brimmed with tears and he blinked them away. "I... um." His voice croaked and he cleared his throat. "I saw him, in the water I mean. I was checking the microphones, and he was just bobbing around like he was swimming. I called out to him and when he didn't answer I panicked. I waded in, dropped a couple of mics in the water too and Windsor hasn't let up about how much they cost. But I didn't care at that point. When I turned him over I could see that he was probably already dead, his eyes were wide open, you know? Awful. Awful."

"What did you do?" Annie asked.

"I dragged him down to the same place Leon had been found. I figured he'd be more likely to be spotted there."

"And you left him?" she said, disgusted. "That's why you wanted to know he was definitely dead, to ease your own conscience?"

"If he hadn't already been dead and I could have done something to save him then, I'd never forgive myself."

"Mr Mold." Annie wanted out of the room, the man was spying on people for money, he'd left a dead boy alone, he was the epitome of selfishness in the body of someone trying to make out he was doing a good thing. "Where did you find Jacob's body?"

"North side of the lake." He had the decency to look guilty.

Swift stood up and placed both hands flat on the table. "By moving him you pointed our officers in the wrong place to search for clues as to what happened to him. You might have even cost Aaron his life. Mr Freddie Mold I'm arresting you on suspicion of disturbing the scene of a crime and not reporting a dead body…"

Annie stood from the table as Swift finished reading Mold his rights. Stepping out into the corridor she bent over double and gulped in fresh air. Her stomach was turning in circles at the idea Jacob had been moved and left naked in the cold all alone. Every time she spoke to someone from Lowan, her feelings about the town diminished and now it was in pieces.

SIXTEEN

THURSDAY

ANOTHER SLEEPLESS NIGHT BROUGHT ANNIE TO THE station before the sun was up. She had crept in through the staff entrance and tiptoed along the corridor to the open plan office and booted up her computer to the Lowan case file in the event she was disturbed.

She knew what she was doing was against the rules, but the need to find out about her mum was greater than the fear of being caught. And she would get caught, there was no doubt about that. Paper files were kept in the storage facility in the basement of the station, but even those had to be signed out. And she was going to have to swipe in with her pass card to gain access to the archives in the first place. It wouldn't take a team of detectives to find out what Annie was up to.

Keeping the main hallway lights off, Annie made her way to the stairwell and down into the belly of the station. It was cooler one floor down, the radiators not turned on to keep a load of paper warm, thankfully. Fire risk or not, it meant there were no staff stationed down there.

With no windows, there was no risk of being seen with the lights on, so Annie hit as many switches as she could to stave off the darkness. It was dusty and close, and the lights did little to alleviate the creeping sensation across her scalp that someone was watching her. She shook it off and opened the door to the archives.

If Annie had been expecting a library full of files, then the archives were a let-down. A grey room full of grey files stacked precariously on metal shelves. There was no frippery or decoration, just the history of staff and perps and everyone in between.

Where to start?

Annie stepped in tentatively, biting her lip. There was no key or Dewey Decimal Classification to work with. She looked at the scribbled hand on the first box and it seemed to be in alphabetical order, though whether it was staff files or crime files, she was none the wiser. Making her way through the shelves, Annie found the Ss and started to look for her mum's maiden name, Sherwood. There a lot of boxes in the S section, and by the time Annie got to the Smiths she'd given up hope of finding anything on paper to help her piece together her own childhood. No Holly Sherwood.

A noise, so quiet she might have imagined it. A ripple of fear wound its way from Annie's belly to her neck, tickling her hair and tightening her scalp. She wasn't alone. Annie held her breath and listened, but it was no use, she couldn't hear anything now over the beating of her heart and the rushing of blood around her veins.

Then there it was again, the almost undecipherable sound of someone breathing. Annie couldn't move, she was glued to the spot. She couldn't see over the high shelves or past the rows of files. But who would be down here at this time? And why weren't they calling out to her? Whoever it is must know there was someone else here or the lights wouldn't be on, and it wasn't as if she'd just turned on one or two and they may have been left on by accident. Annie had turned on every single switch she could find. The place was lit up like a Super Bowl.

"You know you won't find what you're looking for down here." The voice made her insides twist so violently she thought she'd throw up on the spot.

"SWIFT," she yelled. "You almost gave me heart failure."

Annie burst out from behind the row of files and right into the DI's chest. Stumbling backward, his arms grabbed out and stopped her from falling onto the thinly carpeted floor. He drew her in and held her for a beat, her heart racing even harder, then loosened his arms and drew his hands to her shoulders.

"You could lose your job," he said, softly, his hands warm through her jumper.

"I'm going to lose my mind if I don't get to the bottom of why my dad left and why my mum killed a man, though. And I know what's more important to me."

A flicker of hurt crossed Swift's face but he shook it away quickly.

"Come with me," he said, dropping his grip from Annie's shoulders and grabbing her hand instead. "Look."

Annie let him lead her back down the row of Ss and out into the main gangway of the room. He was flicking off the switches as they left each row, plunging them back into darkness. When he reached the Os he stopped and turned and they squeezed down between the shelves together. Annie could hear Swift's heart beating through the silence, see the pulse of his artery thrumming in his neck, it was as fast as her own. They stopped and Swift turned to Annie, his face close enough to smell the minty toothpaste on his breath. Annie's breath gave up altogether. She waited for him to move, to say something, anything to take her mind off the need to reach up and kiss him.

"Look," he said, again, throatily.

Annie shook her head.

"O'Malley, look," Swift said, clearing his throat.

Breaking out of the spell, Annie realised he was

prompting her to look at the shelf they'd stopped at. O for O'Malley. Drawing breath, Annie spun around and started running her finger along the boxes. Oakley. Ockerby. Oliver. O'Neil. She ran it back. Nothing.

"What, what is it you're showing me here, because it's not my parents' file."

"Exactly." He said, his eyes fixed on Annie's. "Annie, there is no file here. Not under O'Malley or Sherwood. Your parents' files are classified not only on the electronic files but also in the paper archives. I said the same thing to Mim when I found her down here… with *your* pass card I hasten to add."

What?

"What do you mean?" Annie said, eyes wide.

"Look, let's get out of here before you get in trouble. More trouble. I had to answer to Robins once already when Mim's escapades triggered an internal alarm. I said I'd asked you to get something, but I'm not sure they'll believe me twice. Not with the case we're on at the moment where everything is electronic and there's not a lot from Lowan or the lake's history that hasn't been made public. You'd have no reason to be down here. We need to get out." Swift edged past Annie, the scent of his new aftershave making her wince.

"Swift, when did you talk to Mim?" Annie asked, trying not to put two and two together and make five. Swift had been acting weird around her. He was keeping something from her. And he smelt wrong.

Even from the back, Annie could tell he was blushing the way the tips of his ears turned red.

"Just before Christmas when I found her down here just like you today, only she was here late at night and thankfully I hadn't left the office." Swift held the stairwell door open for Annie and kept his eyes trained on the floor.

"And what happened?" Annie took the stairs slowly, her head swimming.

"What do you mean?"

"Don't take me for a fool, Swift."

"Okay, okay." He cleared his throat again as the heat of the main building hit them. "Mim… well she tried to bribe me to get her access to your parents' files."

"Bribe you how?" Annie asked quietly as the building was no longer empty.

Swift's cheeks pinkened even more.

"What!" Annie cried.

Swift held his hands up and stopped in his tracks. "I know. I know. I obviously said no. But she's willing to try anything to get the information. Even turned up at my door a few days later."

"That wouldn't exactly be a hardship, though, would it?" Annie said, before her brain caught up. She bit her lips closed and walked on ahead.

"Annie, there's something in that file that was classed as highly confidential, and they moved it to classified when you started working here. I will help you find out what it is, but I need you to go through the proper channels. I can't lose you... as a staff member."

Annie felt her stomach drop. "Well don't worry, I won't try to bribe you by offering up my body," she sneered, feeling sick.

Swift chewed on his lip. "At least I had the excuse of Sophia being at home or I think Mim might have barged right in the door."

Annie stopped dead. Swift didn't have time to think and bashed into the back of her.

"Sophia. Sophia? Your ex-wife is back at yours? Jeez Swift, as if this conversation could get any worse, you go and drop that clanger. Well, I wish you well for the future." She didn't stop when Swift shouted after her.

Bashing through the doors to the open-plan office, Annie felt like throttling someone. Which must have been clear on her face as Tink took a step backwards and held out her hands.

"I've been looking for you two," the DS said, warily. "You need to come to the interview room. Maisie Cooper is here and she wants to talk about her brother."

Annie took a beat to ground herself back into work, then gave a single nod. "You and me, Tink," she said, glaring at Swift. "Let's go and talk to her."

SEVENTEEN

MAISIE COOPER WAS SCARED. ANNIE KNEW THEY needed to tread carefully because the young girl could easily leave as suddenly as she arrived. She shook the anger at Swift and her sister from her head and pulled a smile on her face, nodding an affirmative at Tink as she asked if everything was okay.

"Christmas stress," she said, lying through her teeth and feeling awful about it.

The women pushed open the door to the interview room and hoped for something that would lead them to Aaron.

"Maisie," Annie said, kindly. "You know that being just fourteen means we're not recording this and we won't be able to use anything you say in a court of law as you don't have an adult present."

Maisie sniffed, wiping her nose with the sleeve of a thin coat. "Okay."

"And if you'd like us to call your mum and ask

her to be with you, that's fine. We can go and get her for you. Or is there another adult you'd prefer?"

Maisie shook her head. "No, please don't bother Mum, she's so worried about Aaron. That's why I got the bus here alone. It's just the three of us. I don't want to think what will happen if Aaron doesn't come home."

"Hopefully with your help we can track him down?" Tink said. "I've asked the duty sergeant to bring some hot drinks and get you some breakfast, he shouldn't be long. While we're waiting, why don't you tell us what you know."

Maisie looked excited at the mention of food and Annie remembered what Windsor and Mold had said about the Coopers not having a lot of money. Maisie didn't look neglected, by any means, but her coat was old and tatty and her wrist bones poked out like snooker balls on the end of her arms.

"I don't know where to start," she whispered.

Annie could feel the girl start to shrink into herself. "Why don't you tell us what Aaron is like as a brother."

Maisie drew her lips into her mouth and smiled. "He's a bit of a pain in the arse." She giggled. "He's older than me by ten minutes so he's always bossed me about. I don't mind, not really. We would do everything together, properly terrorised our mum with some of the things we'd do. But they mostly involved teddies buried in the garden, or mud baths being brought inside, that kind of thing. Kids' stuff." Maisie stopped and took a breath, looking around at the dull decor. Annie wondered if they might have been better in the family room, but looking at the glazed look in Maisie's eyes, perhaps she wasn't taking in the paint work after all. "But all that changed quite recently. Aaron started being properly mean to me, not letting me hang out with him and barely even talking to me."

"What do you think he was going through?" Annie asked, softly.

"I thought it was high school to start with, the guys he'd started hanging out with. But the more I thought about it the more I think it was his work. That's why I wanted to come here and talk to you. I didn't want mum hearing."

Maisie looked like she might cry at the mention of keeping secrets from her mum.

"What didn't you want your mum to hear, love?" Tink asked.

"I think Aaron had started hanging around with the awful guys at school because they all bought drugs from him. I think they had a hold over him because of that. They found out and were going to tell the teachers unless he gave them stuff for free."

Annie sat up straighter. "You know that Aaron was selling drugs?"

Maisie nodded, wide-eyed.

"Do you know if he was taking them too?" Annie thought of the track marks and infected injection sites in Jacob's arms and feet.

"He would never touch them himself. That's the

truth. I promise. Aaron always said he'd never dare to take anything like that."

"And what about his friends? What about Leon and Jacob?" Annie asked.

"All I know is that they stopped talking to my brother when he started selling drugs. Even though he is only doing it because we never have any money for anything. Aaron cares about us, me and Mum. It's the only reason he'd ever do something like this."

"Do you know where Leon and Jacob had planned to go away to last week? And was Aaron originally going to go with them, but they cancelled because of the drugs?" Annie asked, something not quite adding up in her brain.

"Mum wouldn't let him go with them even if they hadn't said no," Maisie said. "We're only fourteen."

"Maisie," Annie went on. "You said to start with you thought that the reason Aaron had turned against you was the boys from school, but then you said you thought it was work? Why?"

Maisie bit at her lips again, drawing skin from the edges until tiny petals of blood blossomed along her lip line.

"Do you promise I won't get in trouble for telling you all this?" she asked, her bottom lip wobbling.

"We promise to keep you safe, Maisie," Tink said, holding out her pinky finger. "Here you go, a pinky promise is unbreakable."

Maisie reached out and wrapped her tiny little

finger around Tink's, squeezing her eyes shut and whispering something under her breath.

"Leon and Jacob were working at the building place to make money. They're both older and got paid more than Aaron did there." The young girl looked steely, a boost of confidence igniting her story. "So when Aaron was offered to make a bit extra off the books, he jumped at the chance, especially as it was nearly Christmas as it's always a bit shit at this time of year."

Her eyes widened and she looked between the detectives. "I mean, crappy. It's crappy. Sorry."

Tink gave Maisie's hand a squeeze across the table. "We're not going to tell you off for letting a swear word slip out in this situation, don't worry."

Maisie looked relieved. "Right, good, thank you. So Kirkpatrick got Aaron on his own and gave him a taster of what kind of money he would make by delivering parcels for him. Only when Aaron got them home he opened them, of course he did, he's a nosy little sh… he's nosy. They were full of pills."

"Kirkpatrick is selling drugs out of his construction business?" Annie asked, the realisation of where his money was really coming from hitting her. "The business is a front?"

"I don't know about that, the other guys did actual labouring work for the man. But Aaron got caught up in something much bigger than him. I think all of them did it because they all wanted extra money, but I never thought Aaron would go that low. He hates drugs, always has done. But maybe high school has changed him more than he let on." She blew out air between her sore lips. "It's hard, you know, being a twin in a small town. Everyone knows us. Everyone knows our business. And when we moved up to high school Aaron wanted to make new friends and be a new person because he could escape our real life. I just wish I'd paid more attention to what was going on. Or told someone when he brought home that bag of drugs."

"Maisie, you are not to blame here, and you have done a good thing coming to us today." Tink was around Maisie's side of the table and hugging the young girl.

Annie knew what was coming, they were going to have to call in her mum and make her give a statement under more official circumstances. But for now, they had enough to bring in Kirkpatrick and question him under caution. It was what Swift had been hoping for so why did the idea leave Annie feeling like a damp squib? Was it the idea of being in an interview room with Swift and Kirkpatrick? Or was it the niggling feeling that they were missing something obvious right in front of their noses?

———

CAMERON KIRKPATRICK WAS ANGRY. SWIFT HAD HIM cornered and, though the man knew it, he didn't look like he was going to back down. Kirkpatrick's solicitor was as smarmy as the man himself and together they oozed in the corner of the interview room, whispering between each other after every question despite the fact that every answer so far had been *no comment*.

"Can you tell me why you were using underage boys as mules to carry your drugs across county lines?" Swift asked again, a different version of the question he'd been throwing in Kirkpatrick's direction since he sat down.

"No comment," Kirkpatrick replied, not even bothering to consult with his solicitor.

Swift looked down at the sheets of paper he'd put between himself and Annie. Annie had glanced at them, they were the construction company accounts and, from the look of the figures, the business wasn't doing quite as well as it could be.

"With your business going under, is it just the drugs keeping you afloat right now? Have people wizened to the shoddy craftsmanship of your homes?"

"Objection," the solicitor piped up. "That's conjecture."

"Alright Columbo, we're not in a court room." Swift's face screwed up and Annie bit her lip to stop herself from smiling. "And it's not conjecture, there's a small village falling down thanks to your client. Three hundred people displaced because he couldn't be bothered to build strong enough foundations." Swift turned his attention back to Kirkpatrick. "What was it? Just a front for your drugs empire, or are the drugs a last-ditch attempt to remain living in the life-style you're accustomed to?"

He didn't even wait for a no comment before changing tact. Annie could feel it coming in the same way she could feel when a storm was on the horizon. She sat back to take it in, enjoying the way Swift worked despite her earlier anger at him. Really it was none of her business who he let into his life. Even if those someones were her sister and his awful ex-wife.

"Selling drugs I can sort of understand." He sat forward, fingers steepled. "You needed to make money and that's a quick way to do it. Laundering the money I can sort of understand, keeps your hands clean. Using boys as mules I understand less, but you had access and need and you obviously have no morals. But murder? That I do not get."

He sat back and waited. The whole room pulsed with the anger Annie could see growing on Kirk-patrick's face.

"I'm sorry, detective." The smarmy solicitor broke the silence. "Was there a question in there? I must have missed it."

Swift sat forward again, his face stony. "We found your phone at the crime scene, guessed it was yours by the naked women gracing your wallpaper, but we've had it confirmed, it was the phone you used to communicate with your mules. Did they boys know too much, Kirkpatrick? Is that why you had to kill them?"

Cameron Kirkpatrick's eyes darkened like a

burgeoning storm. He moved his body, languidly, like he had all the time in the world until he was mirroring Swift's stance. Annie held her breath, waiting for a confession, for Kirkpatrick to snap and blurt it all out. But he was too controlled for her liking, almost as though he was enjoying himself.

Then, quietly, so both herself and Swift had to lean in to hear him. Kirkpatrick whispered the words. "No comment."

Swift lifted from his chair, pushing it backwards and toppling it over. Annie got up, placing a hand on Swift's arm. Letting him know she was there, trying to ground him.

"There is a boy's life at stake here, you…" Swift started, jerking his head around as the door to the interview room opened. "Yes?"

It was Page, he looked startled at the way Swift had spat the word at him.

"Sorry, sir," he stuttered. "It's Evans, he's called you down to the lab, there's something he wants you to see."

Swift gathered himself and brushed down his shirt. "Thank you, Page. Stay and read Kirkpatrick his rights. We're keeping him on the drug charges for now. O'Malley, with me."

Annie was way ahead of him, already out of the room and heading towards the office. She had a feeling that whatever it was Evans had found would nail their perp for good and may lead them to the missing boy.

EIGHTEEN

Evans wasn't a man who bustled. He was tall, wide, a jaw that could smash through concrete. Evans provided the level-headed calmness that was much needed in a pathology lab that saw the worst of the worst. But today he was flustering around his desk like a man who didn't know what to do with himself.

"Morning detectives," he said, lifting a pile of papers with his free hand while the other clutched tightly at a sealed envelope. "Please do take a seat, I'll be right with you. Just be... a... moment."

Annie and Swift glanced at each other and sat down, their chairs pulled as far apart as possible.

"Everything okay, Evans?" Annie asked as a pile of reports slid with a whoosh to the floor.

She bent down and gathered them together, tapping their edges back into a neat pile and putting it out of the way of Evans' searching.

"Yep, yep, all good," the pathologist said, still

distracted.

"Have you misplaced something?" Swift added, watching with a crumpled brow. "Can we help you look?"

"No," he replied a bit too quickly and loudly. "No, no I'm sure it'll turn up. Sorry detectives."

Evans ran a hand through his pink hair and pulled his office chair back under the desk, sitting down heavily. He looked at the detectives expectantly.

"Page said you called?" Swift said, a prompt to Evans' failing memory. "That you had something you wanted to show us?"

A beat passed. Then another. Annie wanted to get up and give Evans a little hug, or a shake. But whatever it was that had been on his mind seemed to disintegrate under the harsh lights of the lab and he pulled his eyes back to focus on the task in hand.

"Right, yes," he said, calmly. "Very interesting indeed." He wheeled his chair to the keyboard and booted up his computer, tapping speedily away on the keys. "Yes, here we go. We had the tox results back on Jacob."

Hitting another key, a printer in the corner of the room kicked into life, whirring and spitting out sheets of paper. Annie nipped out of her chair to get them, handing them to Swift as she sat back down. Swift took a moment to read over the results, Annie looked over his shoulder but she had no idea what the mixture of chemicals meant.

"I don't understand." Swift looked up at Evans. "I

can't read what this makes up."

"It took me a while to work out what it was too," the pathologist agreed.

"Is this what killed him?" Swift asked.

"Anybody want to let me in on the secret?" Annie piped up.

"Sorry O'Malley." Evans smiled at her. "Jacob died from septicaemia as we initially thought."

"From the infections at the injection sites?" Annie asked.

"Yes, blood poisoning is a scary one, it swept pretty quickly through his body and his organs would have shut down within hours."

"We found out that the guy that Jacob was working for has been getting his boys to sell drugs for him. Do you think Jacob had been buying from him? Is this what that is?" Annie nodded to the jumble of words and numbers on the printout.

"The chemical compound you're looking at there is a mixture of Carbon Nitrogen and Phosphorus." Evans tapped his finger on the desk.

Even with her limited knowledge of chemistry, Annie knew that wasn't a compound she'd heard of before. Especially when it came to injectable drugs. Where was the methylmorphinan or the hydrochloride? Carbon Nitrogen was abundant in most naturally occurring substances. Annie screwed up her face and Evans gave a small chuckle when he saw her.

"That was what my face looked like too," he said, nodding.

166

"Is this some sort of new drug? Is Kirkpatrick peddling dodgy stuff that we need to alert the services about?" Annie's brain was ticking fast, she could almost see what it was the compound was creating, she knew she'd heard the words together before in this case, she just couldn't remember where.

Evans shook his head. "This isn't a drug," he said. "Your boy was injecting water into his veins."

"That makes no sense whatsoever," Annie blurted, turning to Swift. "Nurses flush out veins with water, but that's sterilised and made especially for the purpose. Why was Jacob doing it? Was there anything else in his blood that he could have been wanting to get rid of? Had he experimented perhaps?"

"It's not just any water, O'Malley," Swift said, his eyebrows lifting as he studied the paper again. "This is lake water. Lowanford Lake water, that's where the phosphorous comes in."

Of course, Annie remembered being told that it was the phosphorous in the water that made it glow.

"Almost spot on, Swift," Evans said. "We took samples from his skin and from the lake itself. Jacob had been injecting water from the lake into his veins. The compound is from the algae, it's what gives the lake its apparent glow-in-the-dark properties."

"Jeez," Annie whistled through her teeth. "That's a new one on me."

"And me," Evans agreed, wheeling his chair across the desk so he wasn't hidden behind the computer screen anymore. "Now you guys need to figure out why a healthy, sensible young man would want to inject that into himself."

Annie sighed, chewing the side of her cheek. "Would this kind of compound induce a reaction similar to opioids if you inject it?"

Evans looked up at the wall for a moment, taking his time to answer. "Would this give the boy a high?"

Annie nodded her answer.

"No, I don't think it would. Obviously there have been no studies on this particular compound, but there is nothing in it to suggest to me that this would alter his brain state in any way, shape, or form."

"So if he wasn't doing it to get high, then what?" Annie pondered.

"He might have been told it was something else," Swift said, toying with ideas. "Something that would give him a whole new high? Something new?"

"Maybe." Annie drew out the word, not quite believing it. She looked to Swift who was already studying her closely. "What?"

"Nothing, it's just, you've got that look on your face," Swift replied. "You know, the one you get when your brain is busy working out who did it, while we all wait patiently beside you."

He gave her a smile and momentarily all was forgiven.

Annie got up from her chair and walked to the plastic flaps leading to the working area of the lab. She remembered Jacob as he was laid out on the table, a young man in his prime taken so cruelly by what they'd thought had been drugs. He was telling them a story now and Annie had to do what she could to listen to what he was saying. She turned back to Evans and Swift.

"I'm not sure," she started, her mind kept going back to the smarmy developer and his nervous eyes. "Think about the first time you saw Cameron Kirkpatrick, what was your first impression?"

Swift puffed out his cheeks. "A man who was trying too hard. A businessman. Someone who tried to look the part. Angry."

"Exactly," Annie agreed. "He was all show. He would do anything to look the part and to pay to look the part, but I don't think he's all that clever. Swapping out real drugs for pond water, that's something I wouldn't put past him on one level. But it's not sitting right. Cameron Kirkpatrick, yes. But these boys? Jacob, Leon, Aaron? From all accounts, these boys were on the right side of humanity. They all cared about others, wanted to help their families. They all had good reports from their school, were doing well in their studies. I know that drugs can change people and they can do it quickly. But if someone said to you, a boy who'd never done drugs before, *here inject this into your veins for a good time.* I don't know, it just doesn't sit right."

Swift tapped his forefingers on his lips, his brow furrowed in concentration. "It would certainly be a big jump from nothing to intravenous. And there was no sign of any other drugs in his system?"

"No," Evans said. "And from the other boy's reports, the one who made it alive, there was nothing there either."

"I just don't think Jacob would risk it." Annie paced across the room, unable to sit down and think. "That's a huge jump. But maybe I'm being naive about what teens get up to these days. I'm way beyond those years."

Swift pushed himself up and walked towards her. "Do you think it's someone framing Kirkpatrick? Windsor maybe, or Mold?"

"It could be, yes," Annie agreed, stopping to look at Swift. "He knew what Kirkpatrick was up to, he must have done. Mold had it all on tape, recordings of what he was up to. Maybe they swapped out the goods for lake water."

We know that Mold has been collecting the water in large quantities." Swift was tapping his hands together so quickly it was making Annie nervous. She placed her own hands over his to stop him, leaving them there while she spoke.

"And he could have just been telling us it was for his own use." There was still something not sitting right with Annie, though. Something that was gnawing away at her brain. "Even if that's true though, there's only a small chance that Jacob would have injected himself."

"So you think maybe he's been injected against his will?" Evans boomed from across the room. "There was a small amount of bruising around Jacob's wrists, it could at a push suggest restraint of some kind, either manual or material. But if it is then he didn't put up much of a fight, and he was injected more than once in each site."

"And nothing that would have rendered him unconscious or sedated?" Swift asked, drawing his eyes away from Annie.

"Nothing," Evans replied. "Nothing in his blood or tox report, anyway."

Swift's phone cut through the stillness and he took a step back from Annie to slide it from his pocket.

"Swift." He answered it and pushed out the door into the corridor to take the call.

Annie looked over at Evans who had gone back to searching for whatever it was he'd lost on his desk. The papers were going everywhere. Annie went to help, lifting the stacks that Evans had already flicked through and discarded and holding them in her arms.

"Do you think it might have been a dare?" she said. "You know, like the whole laundry pod challenge that swept the States a few years ago."

"There is that possibility, yes," Evans said from under a stack of folders.

"Evans, what on earth is it you've lost?" Annie pulled the folders from where they were sliding onto Evans' pink hair and placed them on his desk as the pathologist straightened himself and sighed.

"Oh Annie, I'm in so much trouble." He looked devastated. "We needed three personal references for our most recent application to foster, character references, you know. Today, they need to be in today. And I've lost them. All bloody three of them. One minute they were here, the next... poof, gone."

He made a gesture with his hands, a teeny explosion.

"I'm assuming you can't print them out again?" Annie said, eyes scanning the desk.

Evans shook his head, bottom lip wobbling. "They're all handwritten."

"Oh my god, Evans," Annie shouted, causing the pathologist to jump so hard he knocked the rest of the folders onto the floor. "You're a genius. That's it. That's what was wrong. It wasn't printed, it was handwritten."

"What was?" Evans scrambled about on the floor looking for his references. "What was?"

Annie heard Evans shout after her as she ran to the door.

"You need to check the fridges, Evans," she called back. "I bet your references are tucked in safely to whoever you were working on before the tox results came back in."

She ran out the door and headfirst into Swift.

"Swift we need to go..." she cried, at the same time Swift was saying.

"The phone is back, it's not Aaron's after all, it's Jacob's and you'll never guess who the last person to call him was?"

Annie smiled, grimly. "I bet I will, Swift. I bet it's Noah?"

NINETEEN

Swift drove out of the hospital car park like he had a wish to re-enter immediately in the back of an ambulance. Annie held on tightly to the handle above her head as he circled the roundabout and sped out of the city.

"I think these boys have been daring each other to do stupid, risk filled challenges. Throwing down the gauntlet to each other in a bid to look bigger and better than each other. I think we need to get back to Noah and push him for information, find out what Aaron's dare was," Swift said, hitting the indicator and speeding up the slip road to the dual carriageway. "We need to know where to look or he's going to end up like his friends."

They were at least thirty minutes away from Lowan, even if Swift drove like a Formula One racer all the way there, and every minute they took was another minute Aaron could be in danger. But Annie didn't agree with Swift's explanation of what had been happening and, if her thoughts were right, then Aaron may be in even more danger than she could possibly imagine.

"I never thought I'd say this, Swift." Annie screeched a little as he overtook a lorry, swerving in front of an Audi who was breaking the speed limit on the outside lane. "But can you put your foot down harder?"

Annie felt the pull of G-force as Swift took her at her word, pushing the 4x4 as fast as it would go. The fields and trees by the side of the road blurred into a watercolour of greens and browns, impressionist at its finest. She stayed silent, not for a lack of things to say, but because Annie thought if she opened her mouth, she'd be sick.

"Do you think Noah will give up his friend?" Swift shouted over the roar of the engine. "Tell us what he's up to, where he is? I think they're all dares to do with the lake given the injuries of Leon and Jacob."

Annie shook her head, glad that she hadn't eaten already. "I think you're wrong." She swallowed down the bile that was rising in her throat.

"About which bit?" Swift asked, slowing slightly to turn off the dual carriageway. "Or just in general?"

There were so many different answers to his question, but Annie needed to focus on what they were doing, a boy's life depending on her.

"I don't think it's Noah," she yelled.

"What do you mean?"

"I don't think Noah is the one who's doing this."

"You think one of the other boys is leading the dares?" Swift turned down a narrow lane so sharply that Annie could have sworn the car lifted on two wheels. "You think maybe it's Aaron and he's disappeared because Jacob died and Leon got hurt? He's worried he's going to end up in jail because of what's happened? Or Maisie? Do you think it could be the sister?"

"No," she said, taking a deep breath. "I don't think that's it. I don't think it's dares."

Swift pulled through the open gate and up outside the Brampton's large house and killed the engine. Annie was out of her seatbelt with the door to the car open before the engine had stopped.

"Annie," Swift called to her as she ran to the front door and held her finger on the bell. "Annie, you're going to need to fill me in."

He'd caught up to her, panting softly at her side as though he'd been as terrified by the whole car journey as she had.

"I will," she said with a shiver of fear that she'd got it all wrong and turning up at the Brampton's house was going to do nothing except anger the family. A family who already had enough to deal with if her conclusions were correct. "But I think we've been looking at this from the wrong angle. We've been focussing on Kirkpatrick, Mold, Windsor, all people who have a lot to lose when it comes to money and property and face, at the end of the day. But none of it felt quite right. Why try to kill young men when Windsor could have just given his recordings of Kirk-patrick to the police and that would have the same outcome? Why maim someone when Kirkpatrick could just move his development plans, which is what he did the last time it all went wrong? And Mold? He's just a pathetic little man who does what he's told for money, but really doesn't want to get his hands dirty. No! Who do you know who would *kill* for *you*, Swift?"

Annie rang the bell again before knocking hard with her fists on the door. Swift was watching her, his face pinched.

"I thought you looked like *you* were going to kill me earlier, O'Malley," he tried to joke, then dropping his voice he answered her in a whisper. "Oh god, O'Malley, the only person I know who would literally kill for me is my mum. But, why…?"

He was interrupted as Mrs Brampton opened the door with red swollen eyes and a shake to her voice.

"Detectives, how lovely to see you." She held her body between the frame and the open door. "We're all just in the middle of lunch at the moment, but if you'd like to come back this afternoon, we'd be glad to help out in any way we can."

"Mrs Brampton, we're going to need to come in now, please," Annie said, stepping forward.

Sally Brampton tried to push the door shut, her body failing her as Swift shoved his shoulder against the wood and Annie put her foot between the frame and the closing door, stopping it from closing fully. The woman staggered back and Annie reached out to grab her arm before she fell. Her fingers closed around Mrs Brampton's wrist, feeling nothing but bone and skin so fragile it felt like it should be on an eighty-year-old woman and not the petrified person in front of her.

"Detectives, really," she said, snatching her arm back from Annie's hold and brushing down her shirt. "What is all this?"

"Where's Noah?" Swift yelled, jogging to each of the doors in turn and looking into the rooms.

A flicker of confusion fell over Mrs Brampton's face and she regained composure almost instantaneously, but Annie had seen it and it had all but confirmed what she knew.

"Noah is in his room," she said, sternly. "He's sleeping, I'd rather you didn't disturb him. He's not been well."

Annie felt a wash of pity, a sickness deep in her stomach for the pain that the Bramptons must have been feeling to go to such lengths to protect their only child. But why did their pain mean other families had to suffer?

"He's not been well for a while, has he?" she said to Sally Brampton, nodding to Swift as he started up the stairs. Annie followed behind.

"Please," Mrs Brampton cried. "I'd really rather you didn't disturb him he's sleeping."

They got to the top of the stairs, a large landing stretching out beyond them, five closed doors. Mrs Brampton pushed her way in front of the detectives, her cheeks wet with tears.

"We're going to find him, Sally," Annie said, softly. "You may as well tell us where he is."

The woman's eyes narrowed. "Don't pretend you're on my side, you're just as bad as the rest of them. Telling me there's no more treatment available. Why do you people all get to call the shots, hey? What about what we want? What about his family? I know Noah better than anyone else on this planet and when I say we keep trying then we keep trying."

Swift was opening doors along the landing, closing them when they didn't give up the young boy.

"I'm sure the doctors are doing everything they can for him," Annie said. "It's unfair that he's so young. But do you really think that gives you the right to take another life?"

Swift looked back at Annie and gave her a single nod. Not listening to the woman's excuses, Annie pushed past and jogged to the bedroom door.

"How did you know?" Swift whispered, closing the door behind them, enclosing them in a small bedroom with a hospital bed and a sleeping Noah.

Beside the bed was a drip stand, the bag of biological medicine prescribed by the doctors hanging from the hook, slowly dripping through Noah's veins in an attempt to eradicate the aggressive Lymphoma cancer cells that were slowly taking over his body.

"It took a while," Annie said, walking over to where the boy lay prone and vulnerable. The door opened and closed behind them but Sally Brampton didn't speak, not to start with. "The way he coughed, the over protectiveness of his parents, the gaunt look about him. But it was something Evans said that flicked the switch." Annie turned to Noah's mother. "You were using the lake to try and cure him, weren't you? When we were here last time I saw a batch of empty medicine bottles with handwritten notes on the labels, didn't know what they were at first but when the pieces started falling into place I realised that you were the ones who'd injected Jacob. You were using these boys as guinea pigs for treatment for Noah."

Sally Brampton nodded slowly, perching on the edge of the hospital bed and holding her son's pale hand.

"We didn't think they'd come to any harm," she sniffed. "We were desperate. The lake has healing qualities, everyone knows it. People flock to this stupid little town to see it and be near it. We had to try. Noah's immune system isn't strong enough for us to trial the water on him, but we knew it could help, we just didn't know how."

The pieces of the puzzle turned their final cog and fell into place like the tumblers in a lock.

"You weren't sure how to administer the water, were you?" Annie stepped closer to Mrs Brampton, the sickly smell of fear and illness like a cloak over the mother and son. "That's why Leon looked like he'd been submerged in it and Jacob had been injected with it. How did you get them to play along? Did you guilt trip them into helping their friend?"

"We paid them," Sally's eyes trained on Annie's, daring her to question the morality of what she'd been doing. But Annie had no qualms about pressing on. "Told them to tell their parents they were going on holiday so we had time to prep them and sort out their treatments. Didn't take much money for them to happily lie to the people they supposedly cared about."

"You paid them, you took the kind nature of these boys and turned it against them? Three young men who would all do what they could to provide for their families and you used that. You used them. As a mother of a son who's palliative, how do you think the mother of Leon feels now her son will most likely have to relearn how to function like a growing boy? What about Jacob's mum? She's lost her son and will likely never be the same again."

Annie felt Swift's hand on her arm, a calming presence reminding her to step back from the situation to preserve her sanity. She took a breath and looked down at Noah. His purple eyelids were so thin she could see the rapid movement of his eyes underneath as he lay dreaming. Noah didn't deserve this ending, no child did. Annie knew that his mother was going to stop at nothing to try and save him, because that's what parents do.

At least that's what most parents do, Annie thought grimly, thinking of her own.

"Mrs Brampton, where is your husband?" Swift's voice cut through the thick silence. "And what have you done with Aaron?"

Sally Brampton's head dropped on her shoulders as the realisation hit her. Tears splashed onto her hand as she grasped Noah's tightly.

"Ed's nothing to do with this," she whispered. "He's not here. And it's too late for Aaron. You're too late to save him."

TWENTY

ANNIE DIDN'T BELIEVE IT. SOMETHING IN SALLY Brampton's eyes was telling her it was a lie. But the woman had stopped talking, laying down next to her son and closing her eyes like a martyr.

Annie flung open the door to the bedroom and gestured for Swift to follow. Sally Brampton wasn't going anywhere; she'd risked everything for her boy so they were safe to leave her alone while they hunted for Aaron.

Think, Annie, think.

The Bramptons had used Leon and Jacob as guinea pigs for the treatment of Noah. Leon had been submerged in water with the only other injuries being sepsis and a broken leg. Jacob had been injected with the water and his wounds had shown the signs of infection. But neither of them had healed. The two treatments had failed. Which meant that Sally had needed a new guinea pig and a new way to use the lake water. And that's where Aaron came into the picture.

When had Aaron gone missing?

"What day is it?" Annie blurted.

"Er, Thursday, I think," Swift replied, checking his watch.

"So Aaron went missing on Tuesday, well possibly Monday night. It's just three days, Swift, I don't believe it's too late for him. They're going to be making him drink the water, I can't think of any other way to use it. They've had IV, they've tried submersion. What's left?"

"Probably lots of other gruesome ways to…," Swift caught Annie's eye and changed tack. "But you're right, ingesting is as good as any a treatment."

She turned and started down the stairs, pulling her phone from her pocket and hitting dial. Tink answered almost immediately.

"Tink, we need a crew at the Brampton's house," she said. "And I need you to remind me where we were when someone talked to us about an Ed."

Annie heard Tink humming through the phone after she passed over the order to Page, the sound of pages flicking and the noise of the office in the background.

"Here we go," Tink said. "It was after we'd spoken to Windsor, we went around the lake and spoke to Paul the fisherman. He said, where was it, oh yes, that Grant's wife had ordered him home and Ed had gone home as he had a son a similar age to those boys. Everything alright, Annie?"

"Can you send a car to the lake, and an ambulance?" Annie said to Tink, turning then to Swift. "We need to go to the lake."

Annie ran to the door, pulling it open and heading out into the icy air. The weather had taken a turn for the worse, sleet was falling and covering everything in a blanket of murky water.

"Annie, the lake is closed off," Swift called as he unlocked his car. "There are officers everywhere. There'd be nowhere to hide."

"These two managed to kidnap teenage boys right from under their parents' noses, Swift, they're desperate." Annie climbed in and buckled her belt. "If they needed a way to get to the lake, they know this town better than we do, they'll find a way."

They made it back to the playing fields in record time, running from the car and through the trees to the edge of the water. The sleet was heavier, dropping icy fingers down the back of Annie's neck, making her skin goose pimple and shiver. Underfoot the ground was slippery with mud and ice making it slow work once they'd passed the shingle shoreline.

"This way," Annie said, holding back low hanging branches for Swift with hands red raw with the cold. "The fishermen have a spot just up past this clearing."

They trod carefully and as quickly as they could back into the trees before turning again to the water. Annie hoped she was right, there was nowhere else she could think of where Aaron and Edward Brampton might be right now, but she also knew there were a million and one places to hide.

"So Ed Brampton was out searching for Aaron with his friend knowing all along where he was?" Swift asked, more rhetorically than anything. "What an awful thing to do."

"He was only thinking of his own son, I guess," Annie said, lifting another branch and ducking underneath. "And that's understandable…, shhh."

She held out an arm and stopped Swift in his tracks, pointing to a small green tent hidden in the trees by the shore. From the water, the tent would be invisible, hidden there by the cover of darkness. It jogged Annie's memory of the fisherman telling them Ed was sensible for bringing a tent to the water. Had Jacob and Leon been in the tent when Ed had been fishing? Had they been so close to help but not known it? Annie felt herself shiver, her skin rippling with cold and fear.

"There, look," she whispered.

The tent was closed, zipped up against the cold. Swift gave a nod and stepped out from under the trees, keeping to the tree line so as not to crunch on the shingle. Back up hadn't arrived and there was no sign of any officers patrolling the lakeside. Annie felt her stomach shrink.

"What if he's armed?" she whispered.

"What are your instincts telling you?" Swift whispered back, stopping to listen.

Annie thought hard. These were parents who were trying to do what they could to save their boy, not killers in the obvious sense. But desperate, all the same. She shook her head.

"I don't know," she whispered. "I don't know."

What she did know was that Aaron wouldn't have a lot of time left. They should have taken Sally's phone, stopped her from being able to alert her husband. Annie moved forwards, past the scrub that Swift was holding out of her way. They were almost upon the tent and Annie swore silently at the thumping of blood in her ears plugging them against any external noises.

She knelt down at the entrance, Swift crouching behind her, and pinched at the zip with her finger and thumb. They were numb with the cold and the zipper slipped out once. And again. Forcing her fingers to work, Annie took hold and tugged the zip up as quietly as she could. Concentrating so hard on the task in hand that neither of them heard the footsteps behind them until it was too late.

Edward Brampton came bursting from the trees with a blood curdling war cry. Annie fell to the floor, scrambling to get purchase and move to safety. Swift span around just in time to get the full force of the branch Brampton was swinging in his hands. He fell like a dead weight, blood pouring from an open wound on his forehead.

"Joe," Annie screamed, starting towards him and

seeing Brampton pull the branch back to have another go in her direction. "No, stop."

"It's too late, you're too late," Brampton shouted, spittle flying from his mouth.

He looked like a dog with rabies. Eyes wide and staring.

Annie yanked at the zip and pulled it open, throwing herself into the relatively safety of the fabric tent, the branch glancing at the side of her head with a sickening thud. Drawing the zip down behind her, Annie held it there as tightly as she could, feeling Brampton's body bulge against the sides of the tent. Her heart beat like crazy for Swift, her head ached like never before, and she fumbled at her phone, redialling Tink as it slid around in her hands. It was only then that the stench hit her, watering her eyes, causing her to retch. A pungent mixture of decay and faeces and vomit.

"Tink, help," she gagged, her phone sliding from her hands onto the soaking wet floor of the tent.

Coasting along the fabric on what felt like slimy algae, Annie reached out her hands to grab anything she could to gain purchase. There was a sleeping bag at the foot of the tent and she pulled at the end, surprised to feel something hard under the downy material.

"Aaron?" she yelled, pulling harder at the material until it uncovered what it was hiding at the top. A mop of soaking wet hair, a face drained of all colour. "AARON."

She shook the sleeping bag, trying to rouse the young man, shouting all the while. There was nothing for it, Annie had to let go of the zip and risk letting Brampton in the tent because she couldn't leave Aaron to die.

She spun her body around, pulling at the neck of the sleeping bag, loosening it from Aaron's body.

"It's okay, Aaron, you're okay, I'm police." She listened at his mouth, trying not to gag at the smell of vomit and sweat, and feeling a reprieve as she felt his breath on her cheek.

His lips were blue, swollen and cracked with the trauma of what he'd been through. Beside him, empty water bottles littered the tent, their bottoms gritty with the sediment of the lake water.

"Aaron, hang in there, help is on the way." Annie looked around for her phone, hearing the tinny voice of Tink shouting over the speaker. "Tink, please hurry. It's Swift, he's hurt. We've found Aaron."

She gave their position and dropped her phone back into the water that covered the tent floor, her clothes already soaked through. Annie dragged off her coat and tucked it over Aaron, trying to keep what heat there was left in his body. Brampton hadn't lifted the zip and Annie needed to get out to check on Swift. A head wound could be fatal if not treated right away. That's if it hadn't killed him immediately, the way he had fallen was too hard to think about.

"You're okay, Aaron," she said to the unconscious

boy, stroking his forehead gently to let him know she was there. "Everything will be okay."

She was lying, Annie had no idea if everything was going to be okay. Aaron was cold, his breath ragged, unconscious to her shouts, full of lake water with who knew what microbes that could be eating his stomach from the inside out, it certainly smelt like it in the walls of the tent. And Swift was somewhere only a few feet away but he may as well have been miles for all the help Annie was being. He could be bleeding out and Annie was powerless to stop it because she was trying to help Aaron stay alive, talking to him, trying to wake him, keeping him warm as best she could. It was what Swift would have wanted, she was sure of that at least.

Shivering violently now, Annie felt her own body heavy with tiredness. The urge to lay down next to Aaron on the filth infested water-logged floor was too great to ignore. She could just shut her eyes for a few minutes, where was the harm in sleeping while she waited for help to arrive?

A grunt from the sleeping bag gave her a shock of adrenaline and she lifted herself to her knees.

"Aaron?" she said, her teeth clattering together with the cold. "It's okay, help is on the way. Try not to move now, we're not sure of your injuries."

Annie's brain felt like a cold soup, as thick with algae as the lake. Whatever the Brampton's had done to Aaron to see if the water would heal it, she hoped it wasn't too much for his body to take. An infection like Jacob? A broken bone like Leon? Whatever it was, Aaron could fight it, he had to. Annie knew she'd never forgive herself for leaving Swift alone and hurt, but if Aaron managed to stay alive then at least it hadn't been for nothing.

As her shivering came to an abrupt stop and the sounds of the lake and the sleet started to fade, Annie heard the call of the sirens and knew it was safe to finally close her eyes.

TWENTY-ONE

Two weeks later

"Surprise!" Annie pulled at the party popper and every single police officer in Swift's kitchen went for their weapon.

Swift laughed and put an arm around Annie's shoulders, whispering *I told you* in her ear. She shrugged him off and focussed instead on Tink and her sparkly birthday dress pretending to look shocked at the crowds of people gathered to celebrate.

"Oh, what a surprise," Tink said, squeezing Annie in a hug, and not in the least bit surprised. "And look at you two all cute with your matching bandages."

Tink circled her head with her hands, indicating where Annie and Swift had both been patched up.

"You knew?" Annie said, sticking out her bottom

lip at Page and the muscles trying to escape from his suit jacket. "Did you tell her?"

"I wouldn't dare, O'Malley," Page said, laughing. "You'd do worse than whack me over the head with a twig."

Annie put her hands on her hips and pouted some more. "It was a whole tree I'll have you know. And how did you guess, Tink?"

Swift gave Tink a hug, wishing her a happy belated birthday and handing her a glass of fizz.

"Why would I be hanging out at Swift's house on a random weekday night, when you guys have both been off work for the last fortnight? It's also a couple days past my birthday, and you missed the office party which, by the way, was boring because there was no alcohol or party poppers."

Annie gave Swift a look.

"I would be a crap detective," Tink went on, "if I didn't work it out."

Annie wrapped Tink up in her arms, inhaling her Chanel perfume and coconut shampoo. "Happy birthday, lovely. We've got party games and everything planned for this eve. I'm so glad you're not too busy with your real friends to join us."

Tink held Annie out at arm's length by the shoulders. "Are you kidding me? You guys *are* my real friends. I'm off to find some sausage rolls."

Page grabbed Tink's hand, and they disappeared to the island where the food was waiting to be eaten.

"Do you want to take a walk?" Swift asked,

looking pointedly at the garden through the kitchen window.

Annie was warm and dry and feeling quite peckish herself, but her head was thumping with the noise of all the people and she imagined Swift's was too. There was also a lot she needed to ask him and in a room full of work colleagues she may not get the answers she hoped for.

"Okay, but can we walk indoors?" she said, throwing out a compromise.

Swift laughed and nodded. "Fair enough. How about the first floor?"

"Ooo you're inviting me up into the inner sanctum?" she said, grinning.

Even when she'd stayed with Swift after breaking her ankle, Annie wasn't allowed past the ground floor rooms and often she'd wondered what he kept up there to make it so secret.

"Lead the way," she continued, holding out her hands.

They left through the kitchen door, passing Evans and his husband on the way into the quiet of the hallway.

"You were right, Annie," Evans laughed. "They were tucked up nice and neatly underneath Mrs C and her faulty heart."

Evans' husband looked quizzically as Annie smiled back, zipping her lips closed. Neither Annie nor Swift spoke until they reached the landing and the chatter of the party had died away.

"How have you been?" Annie asked, taking in the huge space with stripped wooden doors and high ceilings.

Annie hadn't seen Swift since she left the hospital and he stayed in for a few extra nights' observations. His wound was larger than hers, his observations less stable, his recovery a little more touch and go.

They walked slowly, side by side along the landing towards the back of the house. All the doors were shut so Annie's sense of intrigue was piqued. Where was Sophia? Where were the dogs?

"My head aches all the time," Swift replied, reminding Annie she'd asked him a question. "How about you?"

"Me too," she agreed. "But at least we both had enough brain cells to lose to still have a fighting chance."

Swift turned when they reached the far wall and opened a small door leading to a smaller passageway, the walls lined with faded green wallpaper. Annie stepped past him and ducked into the passageway, peering on her tiptoes out the high windows. They were in the part of the house that poked like a walkway into the garden. Underneath them, was the ground floor shower room and the utility and from looking up from the garden, it hadn't been obvious that this roof space held secrets. A bit like people; who knew what they kept hidden until you made the decision to find out.

The corridor had only a single door in it, striped

wood, worn white with age, the lintel lower than the rest of the house. Swift twisted the handle and pushed it open, letting Annie see what lay beyond.

"I wanted to show you something," he said as she stepped tentatively inside.

From the bed made with heavy duvets and blankets, the desk, the bookshelves, the wardrobe with a suit hanging from the door, Annie guessed that this room hidden away at the back of the house was Swift's bedroom. Her heart skipped a beat, sending a burst of blood around her body and causing her head to throb painfully.

"Are you okay?" Swift asked, seeing the pain on Annie's face. "Here, sit down."

He took her elbow gently and led her to the edge of the bed, sitting her down slowly. Annie thanked him and opened her eyes to the light, letting the pulsing subside before she spoke.

"You wanted to show me your bedroom?" she said, a lilt to her voice. "Swift, I thought you'd never ask."

She was joking, trying to loosen the noose of happy-induced panic tightening her chest with laughter.

Swift blushed and cleared his throat, lifting the suit jacket from the wardrobe door to shut it properly. Behind the door sat a withered looking pot plant that must have once been tall and proud just like the Fiddle Leaf Fig in the office.

"Wait a minute," Annie said, sitting up straighter.

"That *is* the plant from the office. Swift, if they catch you with that here, you'll be a goner. Never mind your current injuries, what they do to you will make your head wound look like child's play."

Swift held a finger up to his lips and winced. "Don't tell everyone."

"Swift, they're miles away, no one can hear me," Annie said, noticing the fear etched on Swift's face. "You're really worried, aren't you?"

He nodded, rubbing one of the growing leaves between his fingers. "That's why I was in the office early those mornings you saw me. I wasn't spying on you; I was trying to swap out old Fig Leaf here for one that I hadn't killed."

"With Tink's tea?" Annie said, remembering the way he'd tipped the vile smelling liquid into the pot on the way out of Robins' office. "Oh no, Swift."

"It's okay," he said, coming to sit next to her on the bed. "No one has noticed yet, I don't think. But I need to keep my head down and not draw attention to it. See if I can coax it back to life and then swap it out again."

Annie looked at the wilting plant and grinned. "Lots of love and a little sprinkling of coffee grounds. She'll be fine. Or maybe some Lowanford Lake water?"

Swift laughed with little humour. When the two detectives had been found, Aaron's body had been airlifted to the hospital, where he remained to this day. He had been hypothermic and in a state of over hydration. His cells had swollen, putting pressure on his brain, and he was hyponatremic from over dilution of sodium. The hospital staff had put him in an induced coma, much like Leon and his body was fighting as hard as it could. Chances were his body would recover, but his mind may not get over the horrors he'd been subjected to, by people he thought he could trust.

"I'm never setting foot near that place again," Swift said. "Though... don't you think it's weird that Aaron's infection healed before he was found?"

Aaron had been injected with the same infection that had killed Jacob and nearly killed Leon. And though it wasn't as bad as Jacob's, given that Aaron's injection site wasn't being used over and over for dirty water too, Aaron's body had fought hard against the bacteria flooding his blood.

Annie shifted on the bed. Moving her body to get a better look at the DI.

"Do you want to know something weirder?" she asked, thinking back to that morning and the email she'd received from PC Tooley.

"Go on." Swift moved too.

"Apparently Noah was given the all clear last week," Annie blurted.

"What?" Swift's eyebrows hit his hairline.

"It could have been the biological drug he'd been trialling," she went on. "But you know Ed disap-peared after clobbering us both? He was on his way home to tell Sally that Aaron's infection had gone. He realised that drinking the water might be Noah's best bet."

Swift shook his head. "Why didn't they try drinking it first? Why submersion and injections? Leon and Aaron might have a way to go to get back to the men they were before they were used, but Jacob will never get that chance. The most selfish act for the most selfless reason."

Annie and Joe sat in silence for a moment, contemplating the awful choice of sacrificing someone else's child for the sake of your own. It was unfathomable and also understandable at the same time.

"At least Kirkpatrick's finally in jail," Swift said, softly. "And hopefully the Bramptons won't be far behind him."

Annie nodded silently, glad the case had a good resolution of sorts, but something else creeping back into her thoughts. She took a breath and steeled herself.

"Joe, you know you said that Mim had tried it on with you and you turned her down because Sophia was back home?" She started, not quite believing the sentence she'd just said. "Like… what on earth?"

Swift laughed. Proper belly laughed with so much force that the bed wobbled beneath Annie's body.

"Oh god, Annie when you put it like that I sound like a right pillock." He laughed some more. "And you know I would have turned Mim down whether or not my ex-wife had shown up at the door with the dogs and a sad look on her face, right?"

Annie bit her lip, did she know that?

"What happened?" she asked, unsure if she wanted to know the answer.

Swift got up and walked to the window, looking out over the garden, the bandage around his head in silhouette.

"Sophia turned up telling me it had all gone wrong with Kenneth the farmer and she was back to beg for forgiveness."

Annie sat as still as could, daring not to breathe in case she tipped the scales of fortune the wrong way.

"And I let her in, she stayed for a week and I almost fell for it. I almost fell for it," Swift sighed. "But do you know what, Annie? I came to my senses about the same time Mim turned up, telling me you needed a bit of space from me and that I should leave you alone over Christmas. She must have knocked it into me by offering me something so completely ridiculous."

"Herself?" Annie said, still not quite believing that Mim would warn Swift off her and then offer her own self up for the taking. "What is it in Mum's file that is so important to Mim that she'd do that? And why is it so secret?"

Swift went back to the wardrobe and opened one of the drawers at the bottom, pulling something out and holding it to his chest.

"I'm not sure if I should be doing this, O'Malley,"

he said, handing her a file. "But it's my way of saying thank you for opening my eyes to... well, life."

Annie was caught in Swift's gaze but the file in her hand was like the draw of the sun. She looked down at the words

HOLLY SHERWOOD

written in ink along the front. Gasping, Annie opened it and pulled out a wad of paper, too much to go through immediately, but there was one thin sheath that stood out. Annie lifted it, her brows wrinkled, and read the written statement underneath the picture.

Holly Sherwood, current role as undercover in VICE, has been given a written warning for the attempted corruption of Operation Violet. Ms Sherwood has been suspended for six weeks, paid, and will return to uniform work upon completion of her punishment.

A WHOLE PARAGRAPH BELOW WAS REDACTED AND Annie couldn't understand what she was reading.

"This makes no sense, Swift," Annie said, looking up at her boss. "The dates of this report are the week before my birthday, the day I was born. Mum was already married and wouldn't be a Sherwood, and she would have been off work on maternity leave, surely?"

Swift nodded, slowly. "I think it's this redacted report that Mim was so keen to get her hands on?"

"Why?" Annie asked.

"Because she knows something about your history that she's keeping to herself. Annie, we need to work together to find out what is going on because there is no way I'm letting you deal with this alone."

"Why?" Annie whispered again.

"Because this is big, O'Malley," Swift replied, taking the report and putting it on the bed before taking Annie's hands in his. "Really big. And I want to help… because I care about you."

"As a boss?" Annie whispered.

Swift stood motionless for a beat, the pulse of his heart flickering in his neck.

"As a friend, Annie," he said, his eyes catching on hers. "And… maybe more."

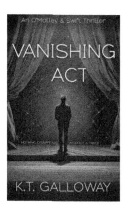

Join O'Malley & Swift on their ninth adventure!

In the world of magic, nothing disappears without a trace.

When the celebrated illusionist, Gabriel Mirage, is found dead in the midst of his own vanishing act, O'Malley and Swift are thrust into a realm where the truth is as elusive as the disappearing act itself.

As the duo peel back the layers of deception, a fierce rivalry between magicians comes to light, and a clandestine society within the community is discovered.

When Swift does a vanishing act of his own, it's a race against time for the rest of the team to unravel cryptic messages, decode ancient secrets, and navigate a world where reality and illusion blur.

But is this world secret enough to kill for? And will O'Malley and Swift find out just how far they're willing to go to keep it that way?

Because nothing is as it seems, and the search for answers may prove more dangerous than any magical illusion.

The ninth and more mysterious instalment yet in one of the hottest new crime series, perfect for fans of JD Kirk, LJ Ross, Alex Smith, J M Dalgliesh, and Val McDermid.

Preorder now
KTGallowaybooks.com

THANK YOU!

Thank you so much for reading Still Waters. It's hard for me to put into words how much I appreciate my readers.

If you enjoyed Still Waters, I would greatly appreciate it if you took the time to review on your favourite platforms.

You can also find me at www.KTGallowaybooks.com

ALSO BY K.T. GALLOWAY

The O'Malley & Swift adventures available to buy now!

CORN DOLLS

Their first case sees Annie and Joe on the hunt for a young girl who is missing. Snatched from her home during a game of hide and seek. Left behind in her place is a doll crudely twisted from stalks of corn.

FOXTON GIRLS

When a spate of suicides occur at prestigious girls' school, Foxton's, Psychotherapist Annie O'Malley is called in to talk with the students.

What Annie finds are troubled young girls full of secrets and lies; and a teacher caught in the midst.

WE ALL FALL DOWN

When a young woman falls ill and dies after a night out, her friends blame a cloaked figure that had been stalking them in the streets. A masked face with hooked beak, immediately recognisable as a Plague Doctor.

THE HOUSE OF SECRETS

With a lead on her missing sister, Annie and Joe travel north and rent a small cottage in the village where Mim was last spotted. Only, the village has a dark history of its own. The cottage was home to a family who haven't been seen in over forty years. Their things still packed away in the basement, awaiting their return. It's a macabre destination for the dark tourist, and the rest of the village isn't much more welcoming.

THE UNINVITED GUEST

Back in Norfolk and back to work, Annie O'Malley and DI Swift are called to an isolated seaside village and the exclusive Paradise Grove Spa. Renowned for its peace and tranquility, the spa and its staff offer the chance to relax and recuperate in a discrete private setting on its own causeway. So when a dead body turns up in one of the rooms with no clue to who he is or how he got there, suspicion falls on the secretive group of guests.

DEADLY GAMES

When Annie and Joe are called to the local park to investigate reports of vandalism, they begin one of the most harrowing cases of their career. The vandal is a scared young woman with a bomb strapped to her chest and a list of games she must play. As the games get more gruesome, the young woman has a choice to make; kill or be killed.

ONE LAST BREATH

After the distress of Annie O'Malley's last case, she's in need of a bit of rest and recuperation. So her sister, Mim, books them on a flight to a luxury all inclusive resort in Spain for a break. But what was supposed to be a chance to sip sangria and reconnect with each other after so long apart soon turns into something terrifying when a group of armed men storm the hotel and take the guests hostage.

VANISHING ACT

When the celebrated illusionist, Gabriel Mirage, is found dead in the midst of his own vanishing act, O'Malley and Swift are thrust into a realm where the truth is as elusive as the disappearing act itself.

Printed in Great Britain
by Amazon